There has been no damage in the ~~machinery~~ ~~gallery~~,
I reminded myself. I don't need to panic.

And there aren't that many employees. I should be able
to find the guilty party. Eric had shown himself to be
good at fixing things, so maybe it was a repair scam.

Of course, Carl was the one acting uneasy. It could
be either one of them. Or maybe both. I'd figure it out.

No need to panic.

Not yet, anyway.

Other mysteries by K. D. Hays

George Washington Stepped Here

Don't miss out on any of our great mysteries. Contact us at the following address for information on our newest releases and club information:

Heartsong Presents—MYSTERIES! Readers' Service
PO Box 721
Uhrichsville, OH 44683
Web site: www.heartsongmysteries.com

Or for faster action, call 1-740-922-7280.

Worth Its Weight in Old

A Karen Maxwell Mystery

K. D. Hays

HEARTSONG
PRESENTS
MYSTERIES

This book is dedicated to all of the Conlan family. Thanks for your love and support.

I'd like to thank my critique partners Lisa Cochrane, Christie Kelley, Kathy Love, Janet Mullany, and Kate Poole, as well as my editors Susan Downs, Candice Speare, and Ellen Tarver. In addition, I need to thank Sharon Zarate and Shelley Harris for sharing their expertise about the business of private investigation and the sale of art and antiques, respectively. I also owe thanks to my parents for a lifetime of unfailing support and to my sister Peg, the ultimate plotting partner. And finally, thanks to Jim, Trent, and Meg—even though you're first in my heart, sometimes you end up last on the agenda. But I couldn't do it without you.

ISBN 978-1-60260-131-4

Scripture taken from the HOLY BIBLE, NEW INTERNATIONAL VERSION®. NIV®. Copyright © 1973, 1978, 1984 by International Bible Society. Used by permission of Zondervan. All rights reserved.

Cover design: Kirk DouPonce, DogEared Design
Cover illustration: Jody Williams

Our mission is to publish and distribute inspirational products offering exceptional value and biblical encouragement to the masses.

Printed in the U.S.A.

1

Why was an *L* hanging in the window?

I set down the plastic container of leftovers I had been unsuccessfully trying to shove into a lunch box and went over to the living room window to investigate. The sparse light of the November morning reflected in the remains of a glass ornament hanging from the window latch. The bottom and left side had been broken off, so that what was once a crystal cross was now just a dangerous-looking piece of glass in the shape of the letter *L*. Fractured crystal shards lay scattered on the carpet below. A small tag dangled forlornly alongside the broken ornament with words in Brian's distinctive scrawl: *To Karen, Keep the Faith.*

It had been my first gift from Brian—well, my second if I counted the strange and now dead plant he had brought me on our first date, which I didn't. And I'd only had the ornament for a week and just found a good place to hang it a few days ago. It didn't seem fair that it should already be broken. I hoped the break would not turn out to be symbolic of our new relationship, my first since the divorce.

Walking back toward the kitchen, I prepared to round up the usual suspects. "What happened to the crystal cross in the window?" I yelled up the stairs, nearly deafening the dog. Reaching down to rub her ears, I reassured her that she was not in trouble, since she's not anywhere near big enough to reach the window latch. Then I let her out into the backyard.

I repeated my question at an even louder volume and was finally rewarded with the sight of my nine-year-old son, Evan, hopping into the kitchen in shorts, socks, and a sweatshirt, with a soccer ball clenched between his knees. "What d'ya say?" he asked. At the same moment, he jumped, flicked the ball up into the air, and caught it in his arms.

I cast a nervous glance at the glasses of milk on the table in the corner. Even though it would have been nearly impossible for him to knock over the milk at this distance, I could feel a spill looming on the horizon. "Put the ball away and eat your breakfast."

He frowned at the cereal boxes and sliced bananas arranged on the table for his benefit. "Why doesn't Alicia have to eat her breakfast?"

"She does. And you're avoiding my question. I want to know how my crystal cross got broken." I pointed to the living room window.

He shrugged. "I dunno. I didn't do it." He tossed the soccer ball into a box by the door.

"Don't throw balls in the house," I admonished automatically before I stepped over toward the stairs to holler up to his sister. "Alicia! The bus will be here any minute." Then I went back to the row of lunches in progress on the kitchen counter. "What kind of sandwich do you want?"

"I want to buy today."

"You're buying tomorrow because I have to go into the office early before I start my new assignment." This was only the second case Dave had assigned me to handle on my own, and I was anxious to make sure everything went smoothly. Since Dave happens to be my younger brother, as well as my boss, I was pretty sure he wouldn't fire me if I screwed up. But I would be back to filing agency invoices full-time while he hired someone else to do the interesting work.

I had never really wanted a career, but my ex-husband forced me into the job market by making me his ex-wife. And after five years of having just a "job," I could now actually see a career opening before me, with fulfilling work, challenge, and a sense of accomplishment. If I failed in this new case, I would be back to just a job. I couldn't let that happen.

Evan hacked at a piece of banana with his spoon. "What does your work have to do with my lunch?"

"Since I'm going in early tomorrow, I won't have time to make lunches." I took a deep breath. "Alicia!"

Something fell down the stairs. I first assumed it to be Alicia's book bag, but when she slunk into the kitchen a moment later, I realized that the thumping noise on the stairs had been caused by Alicia's new boots—dark, heavy monstrosities that had apparently been designed for a construction worker in mourning. She threw herself into a chair and pushed a lock of hair away from her face, allowing just enough room to inhale. "Don't we have any other cereal?"

Evan pointed his spoon at her accusingly. "You picked out the green one."

I peered inside the half-empty box. "And I think she ate all the marshmallows out so all that's left is the semi-nutritious cereal." I looked over at Evan. "Was it green originally, or have we just had this a long time?"

Alicia snatched the box from my hands and dumped

about three pieces of cereal into her bowl. When I saw the back of the box, I remembered why she had chosen it. It came with a free sample CD from some teen pop star with green hair. She frowned as I poured more cereal into her bowl.

"Would you rather eat the CD instead?" I suggested. "It probably has more protein."

Evan offered to get it.

Alicia hit him with the cereal box.

"Eat!" I ordered. Then I went back to the lunches on the counter. Since Evan claimed that only first graders carried lunch boxes now, he insisted on using my plain, blue thermal lunch bag. So for my own lunch, I was trying to cram a rectangular plastic tub of leftover spaghetti into a Bob the Tomato lunch box that was about two sizes too small.

And that reminded me of why I'd given up the effort earlier.

I looked over at the kids. "Do either of you know how my crystal cross got broken?" I waved toward the living room window.

"Why do you always accuse me of everything?" Alicia moaned through greenish lips.

"I'm not accusing. I'm asking." But I had to admit I really was accusing, I just didn't know which of them to blame.

Yet.

"It didn't break itself," I pointed out. "And I didn't do it."

"Well, I didn't either." Evan huffed. Then his expression brightened. "Maybe there was an earthquake that rattled the house and the cross smashed into the window frame and broke into a million pieces." He demonstrated with a piece of green cereal on the table.

Alicia suddenly flipped a large swath of hair away from her face and tucked it behind her ear. "Was that the glass thing your boyfriend gave you?" Her look of school-morning resentment warmed into a look of genuine concern. "I'm sorry, Mom."

Evan grinned in triumph. "I knew you did it."

Alicia tried to kick him under the table, but he scooted out of her reach. "I didn't say I did it, you twerp." She turned to me with a look of almost clinical empathy. "I'm just sorry it happened. A gift from that special guy is something to be treasured forever."

I hoped that was a quote from one of the teen magazines she kept on her nightstand and not evidence of a secret boyfriend, since she is only twelve.

"Hey," Evan called from the window, where he stood examining the broken glass. "Why did Brian give you an *L*?"

Alicia snorted in derision. "It was a cross, you—"

"And it was supposed to be a reminder to treat each other with more respect," I interrupted. "So no more name-calling, please. Alicia, your mouth only has time for food this morning."

"Yeah, I guess it would be a cross. The only time we ever see him anymore is in *church*." Evan muttered the words softly, so I wasn't sure he really meant me to hear.

I walked over, put an arm around his shoulder, and gave him what I hoped was a reassuring squeeze. Together, we watched the leaves tumble out of a sugar maple tree, covering the dog as she lay in wait for a squirrel. "You don't mind that we go to church sometimes now, do you?"

I asked in a quiet voice while Alicia crunched down the remainder of her cereal.

"No," he said unconvincingly.

"Last week you said you had a lot of fun in kid's class."

"I did."

"So what's wrong?"

"I dunno." He stared down at the broken glass on the carpet. "Dad and Linda never make us go to church."

I swallowed the nasty comment I was tempted to make about his father worshipping at Our Lady of the Fairway or the Temple of the Holy Tailgate. To be perfectly honest, I didn't really want to go to church most Sundays either. And if I didn't feel like going to church, then God probably didn't feel like listening to me, which meant the whole thing was a tremendous waste of time. But I wasn't about to let my son know that. "You know," I said finally, "your dad and I don't agree on a lot of things. You do things his way at his house and my way at my house."

He looked up at me. "Which house is *my* house? When do I get to do things my way?"

I planted a kiss on the top of his head. "You get to watch TV now, if you'd like. Since you're ready for school."

"Thanks, Mom." He gave me a quick hug in acknowledgment of the days back when I used to refuse to let him watch TV before school. Did I give in on that rule to buy his affection? Probably. But it was worth it. And cartoons didn't seem to warp his mind any more in the morning than after school.

The painful squeal of brakes outside warned me that Alicia's school bus was turning the corner. I stepped over to open the front door and quickly assessed the number of kids waiting at the bus stop. "Hurry, Alicia. You've only got three kids' worth of time today."

"Well, where are the rest of them?" she demanded in annoyance as she slung her purple book bag over her shoulder.

"Oh, so you're the only one who gets to run late?"

"Yes. They *have* to be on time so I have time to be late." Her voice was sullen, but just before she stepped out the door, she turned and flashed a lopsided grin to acknowledge the unreasonableness of her statement. "See ya."

"Have a good day." I smiled, hoping that middle school had improved to the point where it was actually possible to have a good day.

From the TV, someone with a deep voice was threatening to take over the world by putting remote control devices in everyone's shoes.

Just before I made a final attempt to fit the spaghetti container into Evan's old lunch box, I went over to the living room window to examine the broken glass ornament one more time. It probably had smashed against the window frame, just as he had suggested. But we don't get many earthquakes in central Maryland, so the cause of the smashing motion was likely an act of man, rather than an act of God. I didn't want to accuse Evan, though. I wanted him to confess the truth to me on his own.

Just then he laughed at something having to do with the villain and women's shoes. He was a good kid, just growing up too fast for me.

Back in the kitchen, I stared at the container of spaghetti and the impossibly small lunch box. The container was warped on one side because I'd left it in the microwave too long. Orange stains stretched unappetizingly around the perimeter.

I didn't even want spaghetti for lunch today.

I would buy lunch from one of the shops on Main Street after I went over to the Blue Moon Art and Antiques Gallery for my "job interview." Dave had already arranged for me to "work" in the store three days a week, but today I would go in, meet the owners, and while they pretended to interview me as a potential applicant, I would interview them about unexplained damage to the store's inventory.

I wondered if the Blue Moon was one of those shops that sold collectible Star Wars lunch boxes and, if so, whether they were big enough to hold any of my plastic containers.

After I saw Evan safely onto the school bus, I threw Bob the Tomato (loaded with a container of yogurt) into the minivan and headed off to the office. As I drove through the old, fashionable, quaint section of town, I cast a few extra glances at the Blue Moon to see if anything looked out of the ordinary. I can't afford either art or antiques, so I'd never really paid any attention to the gallery before, and I wouldn't really know what was ordinary. But I looked nevertheless.

I turned a corner to drive down the old, unfashionable, not-restored-enough-to-be-quaint Hill Street, only to find another car parked in my usual parking place. For five years, I had always parked in front of the two-story clapboard shop where DS Investigations runs its covert operations from an unmarked office on the second floor.

Okay, most of our firm's business consists of running computer background checks for employers and doing surveillance for clients who think their spouses are cheating on them, so it's not the glamorous stuff of fiction. But I pretend sometimes that I'm walking into Sam Spade's office, about to be confronted with the Maltese Falcon. After all, I do have a private investigator's license. But the reality is that I spend most of my time working on accounts receivable and proofreading letters typed by our incompetent college student receptionist, Brittany. I was excited to finally get casework to handle. All I had to do now was get the office set up so things could run smoothly without me three days a week.

I parked across the street and decided that the light rain that was falling did not require the use of the Barney umbrella I'd brought with me. As I hurried across the street with my jacket held over my head, I noticed that the shutter next to our right-side front window was dangling precariously from one hinge. If someone had purposefully hung a shutter that way on Main Street, it would look shabby-chic. On our end of Hill Street, it just looked shabby.

So as soon as I unlocked the office, turned on the computers, printers, copier, and coffeemaker, I placed a call to our landlord, who owned about forty little buildings like ours and always managed to give me the impression that every single one of the others was more important.

"I'm aware of it, Karen," he informed me in a tired voice after I told him about the broken shutter.

"And you're going to fix it?" I opted to use my stern

mother voice rather than my hopeful tenant voice.

"Yes, I'll fix it when I paint the building."

"And when is that?"

"After I fix the shutter."

"Which will be?"

"Sometime. I don't know, I'm busy." I heard him yawn. "Call me if it hits someone."

"If it hits someone, their *lawyer* will call you."

"Look, it's on the list. It'll get fixed when it gets fixed." There was a sound indicating either that he scratched at stubble on his face with the phone receiver or that the phone line was being gnawed to pieces by giant shrews. "S'been like that for a year, now," he reasoned. "A few more months won't make much difference."

I was stunned. I forgot all about the shrews and hardly realized that he'd hung up on me. The shutter had been hanging half off its hinges for a year and I hadn't noticed? Even though I parked right under it five days a week? That didn't say much for my investigative powers of observation.

I decided not to mention the matter to Dave.

With fresh coffee in hand, I was ready to face the answering machine. Although there were no calls concerning the Blue Moon, there were two regarding background checks, an offer for satellite TV service, and an opportunity to trade my time-share for membership in a fitness club. Then I got to the last message on the machine and at the sound of the deep rich voice, I stopped. It was Brian's voice.

The pen dropped from my hand and rolled off the desk to lodge somewhere under the battered credenza.

"Hi, Karen, it's me. I tried to catch you at home before you left, and I've left a message on your cell phone, too. I'm really sorry, but I forgot we added a rehearsal tonight. So obviously we can't do dinner tonight, but I hope you can still help with rehearsal. I'll call you later to reschedule dinner. Keep the faith!"

I could picture the smile he always put into those closing words. But *I* sure didn't feel like smiling. That was the third date he'd canceled on me. Evan was right—the only time I saw him anymore was in church. I went to his church at least once a week to help him with a Christmas play he was directing for the youth group. He always seemed to have time for those "dates."

I hit the delete button on the answering machine with more force than was strictly necessary. Then I hit it again, harder, just to make sure.

"What is it?" A high voice squeaked from somewhere behind me. "A spider? A mouse?"

I turned to see Brittany cowering in the doorway.

"Boyfriend."

She nodded in understanding before stepping inside. We don't see eye to eye on very many things, but some subjects are truly universal among women.

She shook drops of rain out of her ponytail, unwrapped a scarf from around her neck, and hung it on the ugly antler coatrack by the door, where it dripped water onto the scuffed wood floor. The oversize sleeves of her sweater hung limp with the rain she had absorbed walking down the hill from her apartment without a raincoat or umbrella. Coats and umbrellas are not cool. Scarves are cool, but not of much use unless worn over your head. Which is not cool. Being soaking wet in November is apparently okay. If not cool in a fashion sense, it is at least so temperature-wise. I expect about half of the young women in Alicia and Brittany's generation to be dead of pneumonia before they hit twenty-five.

As I said, we don't see eye to eye on many things.

The need to be on time for work is another example. This was the first time she'd made it in before ten all year. "I'm glad you're here on t—" I stopped myself before I could say what I really thought because I needed to get on her good side, "early today." I smiled at her even though she was dripping water on a report that was ready to be mailed. While she put away her shoulder bag and arranged her hair, I moved the report and replaced it with a plant that needed watering. "Since I'm going to be out of the office a great deal for the next few weeks, I'm hoping you can take over a few tasks temporarily."

"Tasks?" She was cowering as if she expected me to ask her to train tigers or something.

"Just some of the routine logs and forms."

I thought this would reassure her, but instead, she looked even more apprehensive. "F–forms?" she stuttered. "I thought you might need help with some sur-veillance work."

She wanted to do the "fun" stuff.

I suppressed a sigh. "What I need is someone to make sure Dave fills out his forms on a regular basis, and to add up the hours properly for billing." I held up one of the ubiquitous forms that littered Dave's office, half-sheets he was supposed to tear out of a carbon book and fill out for each period of surveillance. "You know, his tears? I would like you to total the hours for each case and compile a list of activities and draft a preliminary report."

"Draft?" Her eyes were wide with terror, as if she were an animal in the road that was about to be flattened by a car.

"Write. And don't worry, I'll check everything you do against the tears, so you don't need to be nervous." I would have to check everything from the numbers to the spelling of her own name, but at least that would be faster than compiling everything myself.

"I don't know if I'm ready for this. . . ." she said uneasily.

She wasn't. "You'll do fine," I lied, offering what I hoped was a reassuring smile. "And you can call me if you get stuck."

"I can?" Her expression brightened and her eyes returned to their normal size. "That won't mess up the case for you?"

"As long as you don't call every five minutes, it should be fine."

"And you start at the Blue Moon tomorrow?"

"Yes."

"And you'll be there three days a week?"

"Yes."

"For how long?"

"Until I make the case." I said that with a confidence I didn't feel. My biggest fear was that the client would either ask to have me removed or that they would simply run out of money before I learned anything of value.

I got all jittery just thinking about it. "Let me show you the form I use to compile the information from the tears," I announced suddenly to change the subject.

"F—form?" The deer was back in the headlights again.

I sighed and hoped that next year Dave wouldn't simply hire the first criminal justice major who came looking for a part-time job.

2

Later in the morning, when Brittany was settled comfortably into the task of copying and filing reports, I set out for my "job interview" at the Blue Moon. Since it's so hard to find parking on Main Street, I grabbed the Barney umbrella and took a ten-minute walk down into the fashionable part of town where the cut-stone buildings have been power-washed clean of two hundred years of soot, and boutique stores of all shapes and sizes offer everything from custom dog bowls to stained glass flower arrangements.

The Blue Moon, as it turned out, was not one of the shops that had 1970s-era collectibles mingled with antique "junque." This was a more elegant establishment, housed in a turn-of-the-century department storefront, with a recessed entrance and marble-tiled foyer. Long glass cases angled back to the entrance were filled with dark, heavy furniture and hung with a variety of artwork. Some of the art looked old, but some looked modern and out-of-place. A portrait of a woman in an ugly green hat hung next to a canvas that looked as though someone had accidentally dripped pizza sauce on it and then halfheartedly tried to wipe it up.

It reminded me of the carpet in my dining room.

A glance at the price tag, however, revealed that it was worth substantially more.

Or was it? I considered bringing in a piece of my carpet to see if the store could sell it on consignment.

"May I help you?" a girl's voice asked. She sounded like Brittany on a really good day. But the girl who came out to greet me was nothing like Brittany.

Where Brittany's model-gorgeous features seemed to be arranged in a permanent pout, this girl wore the smile of a perpetual beauty pageant finalist. Confident, serene, and bubbling with happiness. This sort of unnatural good cheer usually makes me a little nauseated.

But somehow, in her, it was contagious.

I found myself smiling back. "I'm here to see Mr. Photopoulos. For a job interview. I'm Karen Maxwell."

She reached out to shake my hand. Her grip was firm and sure, just like everything else about her. "I'm Vicki Bourbonnais, nice to meet you." Then she waved me in as if she were inviting me into her home. "Come right in. I'll tell them you're here." I wondered if she was related to the owners.

But her pale, lightly freckled features and petite figure bore no resemblance to the dark coloring and large frame of George Photopoulos, owner of the Blue Moon. He was in the back of the store, bent over, examining the underside of a large, ornate cabinet.

I hung back. No one wants to meet someone with their rear end first.

"Mr. P?" Vicki announced with perfect perky flight attendant intonation. "Karen Maxwell is here to see you."

"Ah, she is? Good." His voice boomed as he waved toward a door in the corner. "Send her back to the office."

Vicki led the way with gestures that made me feel I should be stowing my tray table for takeoff. From the showroom floor, we entered a dark, narrow space with a ceiling that stretched to unfathomable, unlit heights. The only light came from a series of small, wrought-iron wall sconces with battered paper shades. Most of the room was taken up by a scruffy tweed sofa and massive old desks stacked with paper.

"Mrs. P?" Vicki called as she walked in. "Karen Maxwell is here to meet with you and Mr. P."

At first, I had no idea who she was talking to. All I could see were piles of paper and books. Then, from behind one of the piles, a woman appeared suddenly. Her face and hair as dark as that of her husband, but her facial features were small and pointed, where his were large and blunt. "We're glad you're here, Mrs. Maxwell," she said, her voice harsh and raspy, but friendly nevertheless.

I tried not to cringe. I hate being called *Mrs.* Maxwell, since I've been divorced for five years. I am simply *Ms.* Maxwell unless I decide to go back to using my always-mispronounced maiden name. Of course, the more important issue was her obvious relief at seeing me. It was vitally important for the employees to think I was just another one of them. "Yes, I understand you've been shorthanded lately," I said quickly, hoping Vicki believed the explanation. "And that you need someone to help so you and Mr. Photopoulos can work on some other projects."

She opened her mouth to say something else but closed it again when Mr. Photopoulos lumbered into the room, instantly filling it with his presence.

"Er, thanks, Vicki," his voice rumbled. "You can go back out front now."

With a smile and a gesture that almost looked like a curtsey, Vicki disappeared.

Mr. Photopoulos closed the door behind her with great deliberation, testing it to see if it had latched. Then he put his ear to the door as if to listen for her retreating footsteps. He motioned for me to sit down on a spindly wooden chair while he sank into a cracked leather armchair. "Okay, Mrs. Maxwell." His voice dropped to a raspy whisper. "What do you need to know before you start?"

"Well, start by telling me," I whispered back, "if we really need to whisper." I glanced at the exposed stone walls on two sides of the room. The other two walls were old plaster and seemed solid enough to prevent the transmission of much sound.

"No, we don't," Mrs. Photopoulos said flatly.

Mr. Photopoulos looked a little sheepish.

I pulled a pad of paper and pen out of my bag. "So, tell me why you called us."

Mr. Photopoulos frowned. "I told your brother—that was your brother I talked to, wasn't it?"

"Yes." I nodded. "You talked to him when you first called a few weeks back. But I want to hear the whole story directly from you." Clients often remembered information they hadn't mentioned the first time around. And I didn't always trust Dave's notes. He has a dangerous tendency to spill food on the important details.

"Well," Mr. Photopoulos's voice began to drop in volume again, "we think that it might be possible that there's a chance that—"

"One of our employees is damaging the merchandise," Mrs. Photopoulos cut in. "Deliberately. On purpose."

"Why?" I left my question as vague as possible to see what they'd give me.

"We don't care why," she snapped back. "We just want it stopped. It's costing us a fortune."

Mr. Photopoulos looked thoughtful. "Might be a way to make money outta it."

"How can we make money selling damaged goods?" his wife demanded shrilly.

"Not us." He waved his massive arm toward the showroom. "The person doing the damaging. Might be making money off it somehow."

After looking at them each in turn for a moment to see if they would reveal anything else, I continued my questioning. "So why do you think merchandise is being damaged deliberately? Tell me what has happened."

Mr. Photopoulos resettled himself in his chair, which creaked faintly in protest. "Well, it started awhile back."

"October 2," his wife interjected.

"Some furniture arrived from an estate sale in Glyndon. There was a wonderful Shaker-style dining set. But two of the chairs had broken legs." He shook his head. "They weren't like that when I purchased the set."

"Couldn't they have been damaged by whoever packed up and moved the furniture?"

"Yes. But it's our guy who brought it down for us."

"Eric, one of our porters," Mrs. Photopoulos added.

"So do you think Eric is damaging merchandise?"

"Maybe. The next thing we noticed was a tall clock. A piece of molding was chipped off and the case was dented."

"An accident?"

"Possibly."

Mrs. Photopoulos leaned forward. "But then we

had artwork getting damaged. The pictures are all hung on the wall by George personally, on account of them being worth so much more than the furniture. Some of them, anyway. The oil paintings can fetch a pretty penny, especially at auction. So Carl and Eric never touch them. Carl's our other porter."

"Almost never." Mr. Photopoulos flashed a guilty, apologetic look at his wife. "Sometimes I get them to move the big ones."

I flipped to the next page in my notebook. "Tell me about the artwork that was damaged."

"Two paintings by John Tollefsen."

I nodded. "I've heard of him."

Mrs. Photopoulos frowned, her sharp features contorting into an expression of great disdain, as if I'd actually brought in the piece of stained carpeting and tried to pass it off as Picasso. "Of course you've heard of him," she huffed. "He's the penultimate painter in this whole area. Buyers come down from New York all the time."

Since she'd just described him as the second-worst painter on the eastern seaboard, I couldn't see why they were making such a fuss. But I was working for them and they were effectively paying my salary, so I decided it was better not to flaunt my superiority with the English language.

"The paintings were scratched and torn." Mr. Photopoulos demonstrated with his hands. "Each had a great deep, long gash right through the canvas. When I noticed the first one, I thought maybe the corner of another frame got scraped against it."

His wife shook her head. "But when there were two of

them, both so valuable. . .it was too much of a coincidence. And both Tollefsens."

"Well, it was just one at first," Mr. Photopoulos pointed out. "And then nothing happened for a couple weeks, so I called your brother to cancel, remember."

I nodded. "I remember." Dave offered me the case one week, then took it away the next. I was heartbroken.

"When I saw the gash in the second painting, I called the police. But they seemed to think it was an accident. We knew better, so we called your firm back right away."

I scribbled down the information. "Did you report this to your insurance company?"

Mrs. Photopoulos shook her head. "No, we couldn't. They would raise our rates to ridiculous levels. Maybe even cancel us."

"Was any other artwork damaged?" I asked.

"No," Mrs. Photopoulos announced.

"There was another scratch," Mr. Photopoulos said hesitantly.

She turned to him with a frown again etched into her face. "There was? Why didn't you tell me?"

Mr. Photopoulos shrugged. "This one might have been an accident. One of the pieces by Geraldine Miller."

"Oh, that." She waved it away with a short laugh, her face relaxing. "I thought that was part of the composition."

For a moment I couldn't remember whether Geraldine started with a *G* or a *J*. I ended up with a letter that was kind of a cross between the two. Then I looked up. "So you have *three* deliberately damaged pieces of art?"

"Well, at least two." Mr. Photopoulos counted on his

massive fingers. "And four damaged antiques."

"You didn't tell me about the other antique."

"A Tiffany-style lamp. One of the glass panels was broken."

I scribbled that down, grateful that I at least remembered that Tiffany started with a *T*. "Wow," I marveled. "That sounds valuable."

He shook his head. "Tiffany-*style*. It's not worth nearly as much as a real Tiffany."

"It's worth a lot less now with a broken shade," Mrs. Photopoulos added. "We need to stop this carnage. D'ya want a lemon drop?"

The shift in conversation from broken glass to candy was so sudden that all I could do was blink at the pearly ceramic bowl of wrapped yellow candies she held in front of my face. "No, thank you." No candy before lunch. I'm such a mom sometimes.

"So, yes." Mrs. Photopoulos nodded, her face puckering as she sucked on a lemon drop. "We have three damaged pieces of art and four damaged antiques."

"And why do you think that one of your employees is involved?" I asked, looking at each of them in turn.

"We have a good security system," Mr. Photopoulos began.

His wife elaborated. "Cameras on both doors. The tapes show nobody coming in or out after hours except our employees."

I nodded. Normally in a case like this, we would just set up a hidden camera for the client and check it periodically to see if it revealed any suspicious activity, but here the space was so large and the incidents of damage had been so far apart, it would be impossible to place a hidden camera where it could show everything. We'd need about twenty cameras. And that would cost more than the client was willing to pay.

"I'm going to need to see all your employee files," I said, looking around to see if they had a copier in the office.

"You mean the payroll files?" Mr. Photopoulos asked slowly.

"Yeah, payroll, I-9 forms, reviews—everything you have."

His face scrunched into a frown. "We don't—do we have any employee files?" He turned to his wife.

"We have a company that does payroll for us," she explained. "All the tax forms were giving me a headache."

"Well, but they won't have the applications and reviews."

"I don't think we—do we keep those?" Mr. Photopoulos asked his wife. "The applications?"

Mrs. Photopoulos waved the bowl of yellow candies. "I sent all that stuff to the payroll company. Let them deal with it."

"But they probably wouldn't keep. . ." I decided not to bother even finishing the sentence. The payroll company would keep only the financial records and toss out the rest. I would have to start from scratch.

I made a few more notes in my book and then stood.

"Can you show me the damaged merchandise? Pretend you're showing me around the store as a new employee?"

Mr. Photopoulos heaved himself to his feet. "Makes sense. C'mon." He waved me toward the door.

For a man as large as he was, he moved with surprising

speed, so I had to scramble to keep up as he headed back into the gallery. He stopped first at a big grandfather clock with hideous flowers painted on the face. The damage looked just as he'd described it, and I could easily imagine the police dismissing it as accidental. The same was true with the fake Tiffany lamp that he pointed out nearby.

Just as he was starting toward the wall to show me the damaged paintings, the phone at the counter nearest to the front door began to ring. Vicki glided over and snagged it before the second ring. "Good morning, Blue Moon Gallery, you-won't-find-a-selection-like-ours-but-once-in-a-blue-moon. How may I help you?" I think she managed it all in one breath.

Mr. Photopoulos waited to see if the call was for him.

"Well, is it something you can bring in?" she asked the caller.

"Ah." He waved it off. "Just someone wanting an appraisal, probably. C'mon."

"You do appraisals?"

He nodded. "Sarah Kuo is our primary appraiser. She's in every Wednesday afternoon. One of the Tollefsen paintings is up there." He pointed to an oil painting of what looked like a glass of dirty water on a dirty table reflected in a dirty mirror. There was a slash in the canvas running the length of one side.

The painting was hung about eight feet from the floor, behind an ornately carved chest of drawers. The damage could have been caused by accidentally banging something into the picture, but it would have to be a big something, like a ladder. I considered it for a moment. "It almost looks like someone was trying to cut the picture out of the frame and got interrupted."

"Huh, yeah it does."

The second painting he showed me was in an even more unlikely place for accidental damage. Depicting a dead flower clenched in a dirty glove, this painting was hanging about four feet higher up than the first and was surrounded by other framed works that were untouched.

I stared at the gash running down the right side of the canvas. "You'd need a trapeze to get up there."

"We have an extra-long ladder in the back, but I don't get it out too often. Most of the merchandise can be reached with the gallery ladder. See?"

As if to illustrate his point, Vicki stepped out from behind the counter with a folding ladder held in a tight embrace. She carried it over to the far wall, opened it up, and swiftly climbed up a few steps to straighten a crooked painting of a ship that appeared about ready to capsize. It looked slightly less precarious after the adjustment.

"And where is the third picture?"

"The third? Oh, we've taken that one down. But it was there, just above that chest of drawers." He pointed to an empty space on the wall not far from the damaged Tollefsen paintings.

"Are these things all antiques or are some reproductions?" I suddenly asked in a loud voice. "And what do the different colored price tags mean?" Vicki was headed our direction with a painting of something large and purple, so I wanted to sound like an employee in training.

"Uh, some are reproductions." Mr. Photopoulos's deep bass once again faded to a whisper.

"And the tags?"

"They tell us whether the item belongs to the gallery or is on consignment," Vicki answered as she drew closer. "And how much room there is to negotiate in price." She rested the purple picture against a table with enormous clawed feet that looked as if it might run away at any moment, leaving the painting to crash to the floor.

"The tags were Vicki's idea." Mr. Photopoulos beamed.

"I guess I'm not experienced enough to negotiate prices yet." I sighed. But if this assignment lasted long enough, maybe I would get to play a little. I was so used to haggling for a lower price on something; it would be fun to try to keep the price high for a change.

The ringing phone interrupted my reverie, reminding me that I did not want the chance to haggle with customers, because if I was here long enough to become an expert in antiques, then I would have failed as an investigator.

"Karen," Mrs. Photopoulos stuck her head out from the office, "there's a call for you."

"Sorry." I flashed an apologetic grin at Mr. Photopoulos as I jogged toward the office. I was certain that Mrs. Photopoulos had something to say to me and had used the ringing phone as an excuse.

But it turned out that the call really was for me. It was Brittany.

"Karen, we have a problem." She sounded rushed and frantic. "The copier stopped working. All that stuff you gave me to do? I can't do it. And Dave's not here yet. So I don't know what to do."

"Well, one thing you *shouldn't* do is call me on the store phone," I said tersely. "Use my cell."

Her voice rose to a wail. "I couldn't find the number."

To her credit, she did actually sound concerned. I suppose she could have just sat filing her nails all morning waiting for me to come back.

"Okay, calm down." I gave her my cell number. Then I lowered my voice. "And I'm sure the copier is just jammed—it happens all the time. If you flip the front panel open, there's a diagram telling you how to fix it."

"Front panel?" she repeated uncertainly.

"Yes. The panel in the front." I couldn't think of any other way to describe it.

"And that will tell me how to fix it?"

"Yes." It had little diagrams, so she wouldn't even have to know how to read. "I have to get off the phone now. I'll see you in about an hour."

"Okay." Her voice sounded very small, like Alicia's the first time I left her at home by herself.

I hung up with a glance at Mrs. Photopoulos. Though she appeared to be engrossed in something on the computer, I was pretty certain she had heard every word. This did not make DS Investigations look very professional.

When I walked back into the gallery, Mr. Photopoulos was nowhere in sight. Vicki was carrying a painting of a dead tree with something underneath it.

"I thought Mr. P. was the one who was supposed to move all the paintings." I couldn't help but observe.

"He hangs them all initially. But then I rotate them around." She nodded toward the glass cases in front of the store. "We don't want the same paintings in the sunlight all the time. And people are more likely to notice a work if it's in a fresh place, with just the right light and surroundings."

I nodded. "That makes sense. So part of your job is to—"

She shook her head and her smile faded. Her voice dropped to a whisper as she leaned forward, hugging the painting to her chest. "Mrs. P. still doesn't like me to move them, even though Mr. P. thinks it's okay. So I do it when she's not looking."

"What if she catches you?"

"She won't. And I know it's the right thing to do. So does Mr. P. He lets his wife think that he's the one doing the moving."

"He won't expect *me* to move paintings around, will he? I wouldn't have the first idea how to find the right light."

"Oh, I can teach you that. But no, they won't expect you to move paintings. You'll be answering the phone and helping customers, mostly. Scheduling appraisals. When do you start?" She held the picture up in front of another painting and eyed it critically.

"Tomorrow. Is the light good for that one there?" I nodded toward the dead tree picture.

"It's okay, but I think I can do better." She moved farther along the wall and eventually hung the painting over a marble-topped Victorian vanity that looked suspiciously new. I didn't even think the Victorians had running water, let alone fancy bathroom sinks with built-in towel racks.

"So that's the right light for it?"

"It'll do for now."

"Why do so many artists like to paint dead things?" I wondered aloud. If the price tag on this painting was any indication, there was a lot of money to be made from it.

"You can best capture the soul of something when it's dead or dying. You get the essence, the true sense of it." She spoke with the passion of an undertaker.

I decided I really did not have the same passion for art that Vicki apparently did. But this was going to be an interesting assignment.

3

When I got back to the office, I paused. The crooked shutter didn't look as though it was in imminent danger of falling, but I gave it a wide berth, nevertheless. I still found it hard to believe I hadn't noticed it sooner.

Inside, I had to feel my way up the uneven stairs because the stairway light had burned out. Since the building had been built before electricity was common, it was a mystery to me why they hadn't put in more windows. Maybe the original inhabitants were moles.

Dave is tall enough to reach the light fixture if he stands on a chair, so I was relieved to see him in the office when I arrived. He'd been working night surveillance for several weeks and didn't usually make it in until mid-afternoon, when it was time for me to leave to meet Evan after school.

"Hey, Dave!" I waved.

He saluted me with a cup of coffee but offered no greeting.

"When you have a chance, can you change the light in the stairway?"

He grunted.

After I hung my jacket on the antlers, I turned to inspect the damage to the copier. Every door was open, exposing the insides of the machine and giving the strange impression that it was opening wide for a dental exam. Paper lay festooned about the floor in all directions, some of it torn and smeared with black toner, some of it folded accordion style as if Brittany had given up trying to fix the machine and decided to make paper fans to sell at one of the shops down the street.

"Where's Brittany?"

Dave shrugged.

I assumed she'd gone out to get lunch.

"I'm in here." The direction of her mournful voice indicated that if she had gotten lunch, she was now eating it in the bathroom. "I'm trying to get the toner off my hands."

I cracked open the door to the small restroom in the back corner of the office. Plumbing, as well as electricity, had been a late addition to the building, so the sink was situated partially over the toilet and the whole room was hardly large enough to hold anything bigger than a broom. Brittany rubbed her blackened hands under a thin stream of water, scowling up at me as if I were her mother. "It won't come off!"

An awful thought suddenly struck me. "You didn't try to open the toner cartridge, did you?"

"Toner?"

"The black stuff."

She nodded despondently.

I left Brittany scrubbing and went in search of a black mess. And under the pile of paper fans, I found it. Fine black particles of toner saturated the rug. "Don't step in this," I warned Dave as I went in search of paper towels.

He yawned and downed the rest of his coffee while I gently scooped up the mound of black powder into a wad of paper towels.

"Can you make more coffee?" he asked.

"I'm trying to clean up this mess before our office turns into a coal mine." After I carefully deposited the wad of towels into the trash, I began to stuff the torn copy paper into the recycling bin.

"I need to have someone make copies of a file I borrowed last night."

"Then maybe you should call a repairman," I snapped as I yanked a piece of accordioned paper from the inside of the copier and took out a new toner cartridge.

"But you've almost got it working again. So can you copy the file?"

"No." As I stood up, I started to wipe my hands on my pants before remembering that the black stuff would most likely not wash out. I went back for more paper towels. "I have six invoices and a report that need to get out today. Get Brittany to do it."

"I'm not going near that thing again!" she called from the bathroom.

"So get a temp," I suggested to Dave as I started back to my desk.

I set up the invoices, but I couldn't get the hourly figures from Dave's tears to match the database. And then I couldn't even see the hourly figures on his tears because Dave loomed over my desk, blocking all light and air. I refused to look up and give him the satisfaction of having gained my attention. He had it, of course. But I wasn't about to let him know that.

"So how was the Blue Moon?" He yawned audibly as he held his empty coffee cup right at my eye level. When this got no response, he yawned with even greater exaggeration, his foul breath nearly gagging me.

Okay, he won. I pushed my chair back and stood. "Regular or hazelnut?"

"Do we have any more of that candy kind? Toffee something?"

"I'll look," I lied. The toffee caramel coffee had a disgusting aftertaste and if he wanted it, he'd have to make it himself.

"So what'd you learn at the antique place?" Dave followed me into the closet we had converted into a kitchen.

I opened the cabinet, scanned for any sign of mice, and then reached for the nearest bag of coffee. "They think one of the employees is deliberately damaging merchandise."

"What?" Dave snickered as he took a box of mini donuts off the top of the refrigerator. "Do they think one of their employees is out for revenge because he didn't get a promotion or something? They watch too much TV."

As I spooned coffee into the basket, I was suddenly overwhelmed with the smell of toffee.

Served me right, I guess, for lying when I said I'd look for it. I mean, I guess I sort of did end up looking for it. I just hadn't intended to. God had made me honest, somehow. Or given Dave revenge, I wasn't sure which. I just realized recently how often I had fallen into the habit of telling little lies of convenience. That realization was Brian's influence, I suppose. But his influence didn't extend very far yet, because I seemed to be telling just as many of these little lies as I always had.

"You know," Dave murmured thoughtfully through a mouthful of crumbs, "I'll bet the owners of that shop asked their employees to damage stuff so they could claim the insurance money."

"They said they didn't even file a claim."

"They could be lying."

"But why would they damage their own merchandise?"

He shrugged. "Maybe it was stuff they couldn't sell. Decided they'd get their money another way."

"I don't know. . ." I watched the first drips of coffee splash into the pot. Did it make sense? Would the owners damage their own merchandise? But why would *anyone* damage the items? Stealing made sense. Vandalism did not. "I don't think they're damaging stuff they couldn't sell," I concluded tentatively. "The first damage they noted was to some chairs they'd just acquired. Why would they buy them if they didn't think they could sell them? And then why would they hire us to find out why they're broken?"

"Remember," Dave said as he yanked out the glass carafe and stuck his cup under the stream of coffee, "we have to be logical, but the suspects don't. I mean they usually are, but not always."

"I'll see what their criminal background looks like and get Doreen to see if they've filed any insurance claims." I started back toward my desk.

"Oh, can you copy that file for me first?"

I turned around with a sweet, sisterly smile. "I'll be happy to show you how to do it yourself. And don't tell me copying is a secretary's job because I'm not your secretary anymore. Remember? Last year you made me your office administrator."

"Lots of administrators make copies. You do it all the time. What's a few more?"

I realized that as he spoke, he was shifting from foot

to foot like a child in need of a restroom.

"Are you afraid to use the copier?" I asked.

He laughed. "Afraid? Of course not. It's just. . .beneath my dignity as the principal in this office."

"Well, you and your dignity have a good time up there on the mountain. I have work to do."

"Please? I'll change the lightbulb in the hallway."

"You're supposed to do that anyway."

"I'll buy coffee next month."

"You'll buy a kind I don't like."

"Please, Karen. You do such a good job."

I sighed. "Okay. You take those invoices out of the printer, put them in envelopes, seal them, and run them through the postage meter. And I'll copy your file for you." I bet that I could finish the file in less time than it would take to do the other chores.

"Agreed." He dropped a grease-spattered file on my desk.

As I laid credit card receipts on the copier plate, out of the corner of my eye I watched Dave remove the invoices from the printer and deposit them on Brittany's chair.

I wagged a finger at him. "No fair!"

"What?" He feigned innocence. "We've got to pay her to do something. If she won't make copies, we'll have her do the mail."

"Right now we're paying her to wash her hands." I started my last page of copies.

"Soap costs too much." He marched over to the bathroom. "You're done, Lady Macbeth. All the perfumes of Arabia will not sweeten those little hands."

"You want me to use perfume to wash my hands?"

"Please," Dave begged, "tell me you're not an English major."

"Criminal justice. With a minor in psychology."

I hit Dave over the head with the file folder.

"I hope you're happy. I now have exactly nine minutes to run the background check on the Photopouloses before I leave for the overnight drop."

"Why don't you have Brittany run the check?"

I fumbled for a good answer. The truth was that I didn't trust Brittany to do the job properly. But I hated to say it right to her face. "It's my case. I'll do it."

And the search turned up nothing. No charges, let alone convictions. Not so much as a parking ticket. I called our insurance agent and convinced her that it was in the best interests of the insurance industry to run a check through her databases to see if any claims had been filed by the owners of the Blue Moon. And then I had to run—literally.

"See you on Thursday." I pulled on my coat and buttoned it against the increasing wind.

Dave frowned. "But tomorrow's Wednesday."

"And I'll be at the Blue Moon, watching all the employees like a hawk. Doreen said they hadn't filed any insurance claims, so the owners are off the hook for now."

"No claims, huh?" Dave looked thoughtfully out the window. A tree bare of its leaves stood in stark contrast against the dull gray sky. "The butler did it," he said finally.

"I think, in this case, the butler is a piece of furniture."

"A jealous piece of furniture."

"See you Thursday."

"Yeah, whatever." His gaze shifted to the copier.

And I left before he could ask me to do anything else.

4

"Okay, who has the next line? Anybody?" Brian's voice boomed toward the stage from where he sat in the front row of what would eventually be the audience. "Anybody?"

I crawled out from under a table that was supposed to be a box and held my script toward the dim red and blue rehearsal lights. "I think that's another one of Lisa's lines. Should we just skip it again?"

Brian scratched his head, loosening a strand of long dark hair that fell forward over his face. "Lisa? She has more lines than I remembered. Can you take her role for now?"

"I can try," I said doubtfully. "But I'm already playing the disgruntled doll—"

"Shannon's part?"

I nodded. "And the cantankerous car."

Brian frowned. "You're the car again? Devin's missed a lot of rehearsals."

I looked over into the wings, where the scenery of past plays lay clustered as if waiting for a chance to retake the stage. "And all three of the crabby candy canes are out again this week."

A girl popped up from behind another table, and it shouldn't have surprised me, because she was supposed to be a jack-in-the-box, but it did anyway. "I'll read Lisa's lines, if you'd like. And the CCCs will be here late. They had dodgeball practice."

"Let's take our pizza break, then," Brian called, glancing at his watch. "Everybody off-stage."

Everybody turned out to be me, the moping model airplane, and the jack-in-the-box, whose name I never could remember. In fact, I didn't know any of the kids' names, but I knew their roles pretty well since I'd been reading them for three weeks now. If anyone deserved to really be on stage for this production, it was me.

Not that I wanted to be.

Alicia wanted to, of course. She dreams of being an actress. But the play was for Brian's senior-high youth group and she's only in middle school. He probably would have let her help out during rehearsals, but he said it wouldn't be fair to the others to let her actually be in the production. And that would break her heart. So the one person who would have enjoyed sitting under a table pretending to be a disgruntled Christmas present was absent from the stage.

This was supposed to be one of my evenings with Brian, arranged-for times when Alicia and Evan were with their father so my "boyfriend" and I would have time alone.

Alone with a jack-in-the-box, a moping model airplane, and soon, three crabby candy canes.

"You like pepperoni, don't you?" Brian asked as he put his cell phone back in his pocket. "I couldn't remember if you drink diet soda."

I more or less collapsed into the seat next to him. "Yes and yes."

"I'll go out and get Diet Coke, then."

"No, that's okay." I stretched my legs out, an act that

took far more effort than it should have. They don't seem to unbend as easily as they used to. "I can drink water."

He looked at me with concern, and I realized this was the first time I'd had his full attention all evening. This was my chance to tell him what a crummy date this was.

I looked deeply into his blue eyes. "I really shouldn't drink caffeine at night anyway."

"I can get you something else."

"No, I don't want. . .what I want doesn't matter."

"Take that off!" Brian yelled with unexpected force. I scrunched back in my seat before I realized he wasn't talking to me. His words were addressed to the boy who had been playing the part of the moping model airplane. I didn't remember his name, either. But now, instead of pretending to be a model airplane, he was pretending to be a lion, or at least the head of a lion. He scampered across the stage wearing a giant papier-mâché lion's head.

"Put it back, Ben."

The airplane/lion skulked back into the wings.

"So." Brian reached for his keys. "I need to get you some soda."

I grabbed his arm. "No, you don't. Let's just sit and relax for a minute."

"Okay." He sat back in his chair, smiled at me for a second then focused his gaze on my left shoulder. Or something over my left shoulder.

"Turn that off!" he yelled.

I looked around and saw three girls clustered around a spotlight they were apparently about to shine on us. Not that it would have illuminated anything. There was nothing to see.

Brian and I had been dating for about six weeks. He's a big guy, more muscular than I'm used to, and he probably could have wadded my ex-husband Jeff up into a ball and bowled a strike with him. But Brian wasn't that kind of guy. He's devoted to kids, obviously, though he never had any of his own. Not with his first wife, anyway. She died years before we met.

And we really hadn't met that long ago. I was working on my very first undercover case. Brian volunteers as a blacksmith at this historic site where I was trying to catch a thief. At this place called the 1776 House, he works with kids, teaching them about life in the seventeenth century. Or rather, the eighteenth century—the 1700s. I get them mixed up. He doesn't. That's his hobby.

And the youth group is another one. Our life together so far seemed to revolve around his hobbies. I wasn't even entirely clear what his regular job was. He was some sort of engineer, and not the train kind. He knew what my job was, though he didn't at first because I was undercover at the 1776 House. But if he found it interesting, he never let on. We never talked about work.

Lately, we hadn't talked about anything except this play. The group was supposed to perform about ten days before Christmas. But maybe it would have to be the Christmas after this one, since most of the cast was absent during rehearsals and only the jack-in-the-box knew her lines.

Brian had told me I would be his assistant and that we would be working together on the play, comparing notes and so forth. He caught my interest, partially because I spent a lot of time in the drama club in high school. And it also sounded cozy. I pictured us snuggled together in a dark auditorium, discussing aspects of the play in hushed voices.

But since I ended up onstage playing half the roles, it was not cozy, and the last thing I wanted to do at the end of the night was sit down and compare notes about this idiotic travesty of a play. The script, though ostensibly designed for teens, had apparently been written by the same folks who brought us Barney and Sesame Street. Every message was hammered home with annoying repetition. No wonder the teens weren't bothering to show up for rehearsals. The show was inane at best, embarrassing to kids at an age where an embarrassment can last a lifetime. My dog could have written a better script.

And her capacity for creative writing is probably even worse than that of most dogs.

"What do you think?" Brian asked, an earnest grin lighting his boyish features. "I thought the part with the candy canes went really well."

"Except that the candy canes weren't here."

"Yeah, but the way you said the lines, I could just picture them. It'll be great."

"You don't think it's a little over the top?"

He glanced at his watch. "Nah, it's perfect."

"With all three of the girls repeating the same line, it could be a bit much."

"Hey, the show is supposed to have a message."

But if the audience keels over and dies of boredom, the message is likely to have little effect. I decided not to voice this last thought aloud, since he was so enthusiastic about the show. Brian was a great guy. He had a great profile, beautiful blue eyes, and a smile that made my heart do somersaults.

But I was starting to wonder if that was enough.

On Wednesday morning, I had to drive Evan to school so he could bring in his science project, the dog got out of the yard, and I spilled coffee all over my pants and had to change at the last minute. I was going to be late for my first day on the job at the Blue Moon.

I scanned the rows of cars parked along Main Street and spotted Vicki getting out of a shiny white BMW with a large, prismatic sticker of a rain forest frog on the trunk. A smile of recognition lit her features and she waved, but I didn't wave back because I'd spotted a parking place half a block up the street and didn't want to waste a second getting to it.

Stinging cold drops of rain pelted me as soon as I stepped out of the car. I'd left the umbrella behind today, so I covered my head with my jacket and made an awkward dash for the store.

"I was lucky." Vicki flashed me a warm smile as I walked in. "I made it just before the rain hit. Do you need a towel?"

"No, thanks." I shook the water off my jacket and ran my fingers through my hair, which is so short I don't even usually bother to comb it.

"You can hang your jacket in the back." She pointed toward the office. "Mr. P. is here, but Mrs. P. doesn't usually come in until at least eleven."

I made my way back through the aisles of chairs, curio cabinets, tiny tables, and clocks until I reached the narrow room where we'd had our meeting the day before.

Mr. Photopoulos sat at his desk, engrossed in the want-ad section of the newspaper, but he looked up at the sound of my footsteps. "Mornin', Mrs. Maxwell," he whispered hoarsely.

"Good morning," I whispered back. "Did you notice any new damage today?"

A look of horror crossed his face. "No. That's why we hired you. So there wouldn't be any more damage."

"If you want my presence to be a deterrent, you'll have to tell the other employees why I'm here. And that's okay, but it makes me unlikely to find your vandal. In that case, what you'd really be getting is a security guard, and you'd need one around the clock. Both here and in your auction gallery. Is that what you want?" I held my breath. If he said yes, then I had just talked myself out of a job, since he would be unlikely to pay our firm's rates for that many hours.

"Nah, I suppose that doesn't make much sense." He grinned. "So go find our vandal."

"I will." I grinned back as I hung my coat on a rickety coat tree near the doorway. When I stepped back into the showroom, Vicki was talking to a guy who was as tall and muscular as Brian. But as I drew closer, I could see he was much younger, probably in his early twenties at most. His hair was cut so short it was difficult to tell what color it was, and when he glanced at me, he wore a determined frown as if he'd decided I was the quarterback and it was his job to mow me down on the next play.

Vicki did the honors. "Eric, this is Karen. She's new in the shop."

He gave a nod and mumbled something that might have passed for a greeting.

She turned to me. "Eric is a porter. So whenever you need something heavy moved, buzz him on the radio."

If I had been a real employee, I would have asked where the radio was.

Instead I asked why Eric might be so far away that I'd need to use a radio to call him.

"He and Carl are in the back room a lot or in the auction gallery," Vicki replied. "Wherever Mr. P. wants them that day."

At the mention of his boss, Eric turned and pushed past me without any word of apology or any other hint of civility.

"Just ignore him. He's kind of a troll." Vicki glanced toward the rain-spattered windows at the front of the shop. "This is a good day to start. We won't be busy, so I can show you everything you need to know."

Stepping out from around the counter, she gestured toward the old fluorescent lights up on the ceiling. "Now on a day like today, we are entirely reliant on artificial sources of light. So that affects how the paintings will show. I like to move them to gain the best advantage of limited lighting."

She launched into a lecture about the optimum lighting for an oil painting versus a watercolor and I followed her around, pretending to pay attention while I looked at the antiques.

I spotted the damaged grandfather clock in a corner. "Do a lot of people buy those big clocks?"

The sudden change of subject made her blink with surprise. Then she pursed her lips and shook her head. "Not so much these days. Mr. P. said back when colonial furniture was in style, those tall clocks were worth their weight in gold. Everyone wanted one whether they worked or not." She giggled. "Now it's more like they're just worth their weight in *old*."

"So that's an old one, not a reproduction?" I pointed at the damaged clock.

Vicki's smile faltered. "Well, it sure *looks* old."

"Do you think it's colonial?" That, as I learned on my last assignment at the historical society, would make it very valuable.

She shrugged. "I don't know. Now the clock next to it, the shorter one on the table, has a painting by Manet on it, but it's just a print, so it's really not worth that much, and I don't usually worry about the lighting for it."

Obviously Vicki's interest lay in art rather than antiques. But Eric was definitely paying more attention to the latter. Since he left us so brusquely a few minutes before, he had wound three of the clocks and was now kneeling in front of one of the broken chairs that the store owners had purchased from the estate sale in Glyndon.

While Vicki chattered on about the Impressionist movement in painting, I watched Eric as he manipulated the chair and set about fashioning a brace.

"That chair isn't worth as much if it's been repaired, is it?" I asked.

Vicki blinked, her mouth open as if she had been about to say something completely unrelated to my question. She turned to follow my gaze. "Er, no, I think antiques are worth more in a pristine state." She watched Eric work for a moment. "But a broken chair is not worth much of anything, is it? And no one is likely to notice something on the bottom of the chair. People look under tables, but most of them don't look under chairs. And that's why I think this painting over here is so funny. You see how the boy and girl are hiding under the table and chairs? It gives a child's perspective that I find fascinating. We forget how everything looked to us when we were so small."

"Jelly on the table legs," I murmured, glancing back and forth from Eric to the painting Vicki referenced. "When they're that short, the jelly gets in places you'd never think to look."

Vicki laughed, a light tinkly trill of good-natured joy that should have been annoying, but seemed so sincere that I couldn't really get annoyed. "How cute!"

"You've obviously never tried to scrub crusted grape jelly off of furniture before."

A scraping noise caught my attention and I turned to see Eric pushing the chair he'd fixed up to the table. "That's it?" I asked. "And now no one will know it's been fixed? Are we supposed to tell them?"

"Well." A sly smile lit Vicki's features. "All the antiques are sold 'as is.' The buyers have a duty to inspect and make sure everything meets with their satisfaction. It's understood."

"But I wouldn't understand."

Vicki's expression changed. For a moment she appeared to be sizing me up, the way you lift the flap on a pack of bacon to see how much actual meat is inside. Then she smiled again. "You probably don't buy many antiques. But you'll learn, now."

"So we don't have a duty to disclose any repairs to buyers?"

"Savvy buyers will see the signs of repair and negotiate for a lower price."

"So we don't want savvy buyers."

Vicki laughed. "We do. We want all buyers. And yes, most of them are savvy. Most new furniture is junk. People who want real pieces will come here. Oh, I have just the thing for that credenza."

She skittered over to a shelf along the wall, retrieved something that looked like a green football and then glided back, her movements much more controlled now that she held something precious in her hands. It was a ceramic frog. Ugly, big, and utterly useless. I hoped it was breakable.

"Now, Cedric," she said brightly, "you can greet people when they come in."

I thought someone else might have joined us, but she was apparently talking to the frog, because she patted it on the head.

Her smile turned to a frown as her gaze strayed to the paintings on the wall. "There's not as much yellow light as I thought," she murmured. She headed straight back to the ladder in the corner with determined footsteps. But then the phone rang, and she executed a sharp ninety-degree turn to intercept it.

"I can get that," I offered.

But she shook her head. "Thank you for calling Blue Moon-we-have-a-special-on-stained-glass-this-week-how-may-I-help-you?"

She set up an appointment for an appraisal the next day, and I looked forward to meeting the appraiser. I thought I was beginning to figure out what was going on here. Someone was damaging merchandise, it would be fixed, and then someone in league with the damager would point out the repair and argue for a bargain price. Then he—or she—would resell it to an unsuspecting buyer at the original price. Now I just needed to figure out who was in on the plot.

5

Sarah, the appraiser, had conjunctivitis and did not come in as scheduled on Wednesday afternoon. Carl only worked on Fridays, Saturdays, and Sundays, so I hadn't met him yet, either. That meant I'd met only half of the suspects—and it was a small list to begin with, consisting only of Eric, Carl, Sarah, and Vicki. Unless I included Mr. and Mrs. Photopoulos.

It made no sense to include them, since they'd hired me. But then, the whole vandalism thing made no sense. So adding them to the list made as much sense as anything else. As I drove into the office on Thursday, I started mentally composing the notes I would add to my activity report. Before Dave arrived, I would have my report finished, have run background checks on the Blue Moon employees, and have started training Brittany on all of the office equipment.

In the mornings, I'm usually—which means always—the first one to arrive. I turn on the lights and equipment, make coffee, and have time to adjust before I need to talk to anyone. But not today. Dave was right there when I opened the door. Wearing a tie.

"Who died?" I asked breathlessly, as I clutched at my lunch box full of leftovers.

But if he was dressed for a funeral, it was someone he didn't mind losing. He wore the sort of smile I wasn't accustomed to seeing at this hour from him or anyone else except the guy who roasts coffee at Bean Hollow, and I figured there was so much caffeine in the air at that coffeehouse that it kept everyone perpetually perky.

"Hey, Karen!" He hurried over to me, displaying pants with a crease and no spills, and polished loafers in place of his usual black gym shoes. "There's someone I'd like you to meet." He put his arm around me and ushered me over to the corner, where I assumed I'd meet a bereaved member of some client's family. A tall, skinny guy, dressed in a dark suit with a steel gray shirt and nondescript tie, stood in the corner, apparently examining the acoustical tiles in the ceiling. The posture accentuated his long nose, as did his short hair and small octagonal glasses.

I put on what I hoped was a sympathetic smile.

"Rodney, this is Karen. The one I told you about."

Something about the knowing look he flashed Rodney sent up warning flags in my head.

As Rodney focused his gaze on me, I took a step back. "Dave, you know I'm already dating someone," I hissed out of the corner of my mouth. He'd tried to trap me like this before but never in the office.

"Rodney is the office maximizer," Dave announced with pride. "Since you'll be out of the office so much now, I decided we needed to bring in some help."

Rodney reached out to shake my hand with some reluctance, as if regretting the fact that one of us was not wearing gloves. "How do you do, Mrs. Maxwell? I'm Rodney Cadle."

I suddenly felt more awkward than if this actually had been a blind date. He gave the impression that he was evaluating everything about me, from my messy hair to my mud-spattered shoes. His hand was cold and clammy, so it was a relief that he let go of mine quickly.

I cleared my throat. "I'm Karen Maxwell. But I guess you already know that."

"A pleasure to meet you at last, Mrs. Maxwell."

"Karen," Dave and I said at once.

Rodney's forehead creased in a frown of disapproval. "To keep a professional tone, we need to avoid falling into the trap of over-familiarity. Just because every telemarketer on the planet feels free to address you by your first name, doesn't mean we approve."

"We don't approve of first names?" I asked dubiously.

"Not during working hours, Mrs. Maxwell. Mr. Sarkesian has agreed that we need to raise the tone of this office to an urban professional level."

Dave nodded. "We'll be competing with firms from Washington and Baltimore."

I looked at Dave. "But Dave, you've never wanted to—"

Rodney shook his head. "Mr. Sarkesian."

"He's my brother."

"Not in front of clients."

I waved around the office. "I don't see any clients."

"A professional tone is not something you turn off and on like a faucet, Mrs. Maxwell. It requires constant maintenance. And a client may arrive unannounced at any moment."

"Well no, actually, they can't. We keep the door locked. We don't want the unhappy relatives of any clients to arrive unannounced at any moment. They ring downstairs, and we decide whether or not to let them in."

Rodney, or perhaps I should say Mr. Cadle, raised an eyebrow. "An archaic, melodramatic practice. The public is entering a professional business establishment, not a speakeasy."

"You want to keep the door unlocked? Fine." I turned to Dave. "Put his desk closest to the door and I'll move mine to the closet. Do we have any bulletproof glass?"

Dave did this thing where he twisted his mouth sideways, which meant that he was thinking, or at least pretending to. "We had a sample piece in the closet, but I haven't seen it for a while."

I started for the closet. "I hope you didn't give it to Brittany for show-and-tell."

Rodney marched after me. "I've already cleaned out the closet, Mrs. Maxwell. I'm afraid you won't find any samples."

The closet was indeed empty of samples and almost everything else. The extra pair of boots I kept, toner cartridges waiting to be recycled, Dave's spare set of golf clubs, a sweater that we think belonged to the intern we had before Brittany, a broken but still useful umbrella, and all the other miscellaneous junk that we'd stuffed into the long narrow confines of that closet—it was all gone. "Well, I guess I can move right in," I said slowly. What had that man done with my boots? He had no right to throw away other people's belongings.

"Mr. Sarkesian told me you didn't need any of the trash in there. So I'm planning to use that space for the mailing station."

"But we like to keep the postage scale out here, where we can read it. There's no light in that closet."

"An electrician is coming tomorrow."

"Did you authorize that, Dave?"

"Mr. Sarkesian."

I ignored Mr. Cadle and continued to address my brother. "Mucking with the electricity in an old building like this is expensive."

Dave shrugged as he sauntered over toward us. "We had to have him come out to fix the light in the stairwell."

"We're hiring an electrician to change a lightbulb?" I sputtered in disbelief.

Rodney affixed an obsequious smile on his face, as if he'd been hired to placate the restless natives in a nursing home. "It's not our job to determine the best means to fix the light. Our expertise is in different realms. It would be a waste of time for Mr. Sarkesian, the investigative professional, to spend his time on other business. We keep our professionals engaged in the jobs for which they've been trained. That's how to maximize efficiency."

"Are you ready to pay for this new efficiency?" I leaned over to ask Dave softly. "Do we really need to pay a guy to clean out our closets and hire electricians for us?"

He nodded. "You told me to hire somebody."

I decided Mr. Cadle was probably getting a kickback from the electrician. But I held my tongue. This guy was annoying. But he wouldn't last. Once Dave realized how much it was costing the firm, Rodney Cadle would be out on his ear.

Friday was clear and warmer than it had been for weeks, so shoppers and coffee shop patrons had already laid claim to the best parking spots on Main Street by the time I arrived at the Blue Moon. I would probably become quite proficient at parallel parking before the assignment was over. But I wasn't enjoying the learning process. My only consolation was that my children weren't there to witness my embarrassment.

I made it in before Vicki today, but she drove up just as I crossed the street, and she zipped her little BMW into a parking space with an agility I could never hope to match, at least not in a minivan.

"Good morning!" Even her voice was smiling. I wondered if having enough money to buy a BMW would automatically put someone in a good mood.

Since I drive a minivan that smells like spilled coffee and old sweatsocks, my mood was somewhat less gracious as I held open the door for her. Eric stuck his head out from the back when he heard Vicki's greeting. I waved at him, but he didn't acknowledge my presence, so I decided that on the scale of morning rudeness, I didn't rank at the absolute bottom. He nodded to Vicki and disappeared back into his lair.

"Do we have two porters in today?" I was anxious to meet Carl and a little concerned when I realized that Eric was already here.

"Maybe. We have an auction shipment due in today, so they may have put both guys on the schedule. Let me check." She flung what appeared to be a designer handbag into a drawer under the counter and then grabbed a notebook next to the cash register. "Yes," she said as she scanned the front page of the book. "Carl is on the schedule."

"I thought he worked every Friday."

"Oh, no. He's only as needed. He works at the firehouse on Route 103, so this is just an extra job for him."

Thank you, Vicki. Now I knew where to find him if I needed him. People are usually a lot more open to questioning at work than at home. I can see why—I'd feel pretty creepy knowing someone had followed me home or gotten ahold of personal records with my address.

"Have you seen the new postmodern exhibit at the Walters?" Vicki asked suddenly as she shut the notebook and dropped it back into place. "I felt as though I could touch the artists' thoughts. It gave me some great ideas." She started off toward the nearest wall of paintings without giving me a chance to answer.

Maybe she's used to having conversations with Eric.

While I tried to think up an excuse to go talk to Carl in the auction gallery, I examined the undersides of a few chairs to see if any of them showed signs of repair.

"Uh-oh, I hope Mrs. P. isn't in early today," I heard Vicki mutter nearby.

I looked up to see Vicki eyeing the walls as she clutched a painting I'd seen before, the one with a dead tree on it. I looked at it more closely this time, and saw that underneath the tree, there was something that appeared to be either a pile of dirty laundry or a guy wearing a lot of clothes all at once. Like a homeless person. The whole painting depicted a sense of hopeless, timeless cold and despair. It was a sad painting. But the more I looked at it, the more I liked the way it touched me. "Is that a Tollefsen?" I asked. The painting shared the same shapelessness and same somber colors as the damaged paintings Mr. Photopoulos had shown me.

Vicki shook her head. "Oh no." She moved her arm so that I could see the artist's name painted in small but bold letters in the right lower corner. *Freels.*

"Do we have any others of his? Or hers?" I don't know why I assume most artists are men.

"It's a he. Craig Freels. And no, right now this is the only one."

At the sound of the door opening, she nearly dropped the painting.

"Do you want me to put it back where it was?" I offered.

She shook her head. "There isn't time," she whispered. She nodded toward a small picture on the wall near me. "Take that one down, quick."

I did as she asked and she hung the Freels picture in its place, even though it was bigger and overlapped a neighboring portrait of a woman leaning over a muddy pond. Then she yanked the small picture from my hands, set it on a chair, and pushed the chair up to a table. She stepped in front of the chair. "Good morning, Mrs. P." She smiled as if she was actually pleased to see her boss.

"G'morning, girls." Mrs. Photopoulos walked with a slow, uneven gait, a shapeless leather bag across one shoulder and a paper shopping bag in the other hand. "I brought some pumpkin muffins in, so make sure you come back to the office and get one while they're still hot." She offered a smile of genuine warmth, and I immediately felt guilty for trying to deceive her about moving paintings, even though I really didn't think we were doing anything wrong.

"Thank you, we will," Vicki said quickly. "I was just

showing Karen how we inventory the chairs when they're in sets."

"Oh, good. Is Sarah coming in today?"

"She hasn't called yet."

Mrs. Photopoulos nodded. "Don't forget to reschedule her appointments," she added as she toddled back toward the office.

"I took care of it yesterday."

"Yesterday?" I asked with surprise. "Are you here every day? Don't you ever have to go to class?"

"Oh, I'm not in school. I finished last year. My bachelor's and master's, a joint program. Art history and resource management."

And she was working for minimum wage in a no-name gallery in Ellicott City? That must be a disappointment. She had probably envisioned working in the master galleries at the Smithsonian or the Met. Instead, it was grandfather clocks and oil paintings of muddy ponds. "That's great," I said, trying to muster enthusiasm. So where did she get the money for the BMW and fancy handbag?

The bell at the door jingled as two women walked into the shop.

"Can I watch while you wait on them?" I asked quickly.

She grinned. "Sure." She glided over to the women, who looked to be in their late forties or fifties. "May I help you find anything today?" she offered.

"I'm looking for Italian," answered the taller of the two, a woman with bright eyes and short salt-and-pepper hair.

"Italian. . .furniture?"

The woman turned to her companion and laughed. "Italian everything. I just got back from a trip to Italy and my house seems so cold. I need some of that warmth."

Vicki nodded. "So you're looking for pieces to evoke the sense of *amichevole*."

"Isn't that a red wine?" the shorter woman asked.

Her companion and Vicki took it for a joke and laughed, but the confused look on the other woman's face seemed to indicate that she was seriously concerned that her friend wanted to decorate her home in red wine.

Vicki's smile remained friendly, but her tone grew businesslike. "I'd recommend starting with one room, the room where you spend the most time perhaps. Find a couple of simple pieces as foundation, and then focus on the walls, which are the first thing you see when you walk into the room. New artwork, perhaps a landscape or two, will really change the feel of the room and bring in that warmth."

I would have suggested a space heater, which is the reason I would never make a living as a salesperson, at least not here.

I followed along as Vicki showed the Italian vacationer some shabby-chic furniture that was designed to evoke the crumbling villa look. But instead of paying attention to her sales techniques, I was still looking for signs of furniture repairs. I glanced at the paintings, too, although I wasn't sure it was possible to fully repair ripped canvas. The torn Tollefsen prints had been taped together in the back, but the rips were obvious on close inspection. The torn print by Geraldine Miller had been replaced with a surrealistic depiction of a hairdryer, a new Tollefsen. It wasn't until then that I realized just how many of the gallery's paintings had been done by that local artist. No wonder Mrs. Photopoulos defended him so strongly. His reputation set the value for about half of their inventory.

The Italian vacationer and her friend weren't terribly interested in the furniture or the paintings Vicki showed them, but they liked a marble bust on a stand near the back of the store. I decided it might just possibly be even uglier than Cedric the ceramic frog. But it didn't matter for long, because the piece was purchased and wrapped before I could make up my mind.

Vicki pulled a radio from behind the counter and used it to call one of the porters. She received a grunt in response. I assumed it was Eric who had answered. A minute later he appeared in the showroom. He maneuvered the wrapped marble onto a dolly with obvious difficulty but in silence, with no cursing or complaint. Then, with a flash of a smile toward Vicki, he wheeled the thing out to the buyer's car.

"It's nice of him to do that," I murmured, watching him strain to hoist the bust into the backseat.

"It's his job," Vicki said matter-of-factly.

"The last time I bought something heavy, no one in the store would lift a finger to help me with it unless I paid for their delivery service."

"That's tacky."

"I think I used stronger language."

Eric's face was red when he stepped back inside the shop.

"Good work," I murmured.

He mumbled something in response that I took for a "thank you."

I expected him to immediately disappear into the back or to the auction gallery or wherever else he usually disappeared to. But instead he paused to pick up a small table made of dark wood. Or rather I guess it was only covered in a veneer of dark wood, because a long wedge-shaped piece of that veneer was missing, and a light wood showed through underneath. He carried the table out the back door of the showroom.

"Will I ever need to do any work in the auction gallery?" I asked Vicki somewhat wistfully.

She shook her head. "It's only open on Sundays, when you're not here."

I felt an immediate flash of guilt. The weekends were the busiest days for the gallery, and I had refused to work them. My first assignment had required me to work every Saturday and I didn't want to get stuck with that again. I told Dave that I was more likely to learn about employee activities during the quiet hours than during the busy ones. But I had no idea if that were true.

In any case, I probably did need to check out the auction gallery, even if none of the damage had occurred there. And I certainly needed to meet Carl. *And* I needed to see what Eric was doing in the back with the table he carried out.

I waved toward the back door. "Is there a way to get to the auction gallery from back there?"

"Yes." Vicki nodded, her thin, silver earrings flashing as they caught the light. "That's the fastest way, actually."

I licked my lips. "Do you think Mr. and Mrs. P. would mind if I ran back real quick to take a look?"

"As long as we're not busy, no."

"Okay, great." I had already bounded several steps away before I realized that the gallery doors were probably locked. "One of the porters can let me in, right?"

"Yes. Well," Vicki grinned "just say you're me."

"I'm you?"

"Eric would push his own mother out of a lifeboat if it would make room for Vicki." Mrs. P.'s voice came from somewhere behind me. She must have just stepped out of the office. "He's been madly in love with her since the first day she set foot in the shop."

Vicki's face flushed a becoming shade of pink. "Stop, now, Mrs. P. You're embarrassing me. Eric's just a really nice guy."

"Who would do anything for you. Now, don't worry." She held up a hand to fend off any further objections from Vicki. "I know you're not interested in him like that; I'm not trying to pressure you. Just trying to explain to Karen."

At first I thought she might have been surreptitiously trying to tell me something, but the teasing smile she lavished on Vicki made it seem like she wasn't really trying to tell *me* anything at all. She obviously thought Vicki should give the guy a chance.

Vicki, who just two days before referred to Eric as "a troll."

Beauty-and-the-beast scenarios only work in Hollywood, where the beast is really a beauty covered in makeup. But in real life, Eric had about as much chance of getting a date with Vicki as my son Evan would.

"So you wanna see the auction gallery?" Mrs. P. nodded toward the back. "I'll take you over."

"Uh, thanks." I tried to look grateful. But I doubted Eric and Carl would say much around their boss, so my opportunity to learn anything was now substantially reduced.

Even without the load of shopping bags she carried in every morning, Mrs. P. still shuffled when she walked, but it was now a faster shuffle, accented by the jingle from a collection of keys clipped to the belt loop of her skirt. She led me through the back door of the showroom to a small room, with a low slanted ceiling that looked like a storage shed someone had tacked onto the building as an afterthought. The room had no heat or windows; uncovered bulbs screwed into the ceiling fixtures provided the only illumination for a collection of chairs with missing seats, a dresser with veneer curling up like waves at the beach, and a desk that looked like it had been crudely sawed in half as part of an incompetent magician's trick. A worn church pew with a split seat lined the back wall; it served as a shelf to hold an array of hammers, saws, files, paint, wax, and other woodworking items.

Eric was not there, so he must have gone over to the auction gallery.

Mrs. P. flung open the door and ushered me out into the sunshine.

It was a short walk across the back lot to the auction gallery. From the back, all the buildings looked plain, and it was hard to guess what kind of businesses they housed. The auction gallery looked to be maybe a little wider than the others, but the windows had been painted black, so it gave the place a dead, dreary look.

With practiced ease, Mrs. P. unclipped the ring of keys from her waist, flipped to one that looked exactly like all the others to my untrained eye, and inserted it into the lock. It clicked open obligingly as she turned it, and we stepped into a cavernous room lit only at the back, where Eric was holding up a large round mirror while another man, taller and not as slump-shouldered as Eric, appeared to be attaching it to an old marble-topped dresser.

"Whoa, Mrs. P.," the other man called as he looked up and saw us. "They didn't have to send you over, too. I just needed *one* extra pair of hands." He was smiling as if he was trying to make a joke, but he looked uneasy, too. Almost worried.

"It's good to see you, too, Carl," she teased.

"No, really, the mirror's not all that heavy, but it's fragile, y'know?" Carl flipped a shock of dirty-looking brown hair out of his eyes. "So, like, I wanted someone to hold it steady while I tightened the screws. But I can manage the rest of this by myself."

"It's no problem for Eric to help," Mrs. P. reassured him. "That's why I put you both on the schedule today. The Ryland estate has a lot of heavy pieces."

"No, but I can manage. You didn't need to come check. I would have radioed if I needed more help."

"I'm just here to show the gallery to the new girl." She nodded toward me.

Both men looked at me for a moment as if they expected me to perform or do something spectacular to have justified dragging their boss all this way.

I figured I could at least introduce myself. "Hi. I'm Karen."

Carl held out a clean hand with dirty fingernails. "Carl," he said simply as he shook my hand with a firm grip. He might have been nervous about seeing his boss, but he seemed to have no uneasiness about me. "You can call me anytime you need something moved." His face reddened. "Any day I'm here, that is."

"We're getting into a busier season now, so we'll be able to schedule you more often," Mrs. P. said quickly.

"S'getting heavy," Eric huffed.

I think we'd all forgotten that he was still holding the mirror.

"Oh yeah, hope you'll excuse me, ladies, can't leave a job half done, y'know." Carl immediately went back to work with a screwdriver.

And Mrs. P. dragged me over to a stack of ugly brown throw rugs that I wouldn't have paid five bucks for at a yard sale. "Take a good look at these, Karen," she gushed with enthusiasm. "You won't see the like again for a long while. These are all original Navajos."

"Uh, great." I assumed she meant that they'd been made by Navajo Indians, not that they were flattened Native Americans.

"We've got two phone bidders scheduled for Sunday. Collectors. And that's in addition to whoever's here in person. We expect to get thousands for each one."

"So these are popular, huh?"

"Very."

I had a sudden horrifying vision of Eric or Carl cutting through one with a box cutter. I almost asked Mrs. P. if she was ever worried about something happening to valuable merchandise. But of course she was. That's why she had hired me. I was supposed to keep these things safe from Eric and Carl and whoever else might rip into them.

The place was so big. And I was just one part-time set

of eyes. How could I possibly do it?

There has been no damage at the auction gallery, I reminded myself. I don't need to panic.

And there aren't that many employees. I should be able to find the guilty party. Eric had shown himself to be good at fixing things, so maybe it was a repair scam.

Of course, Carl was the one acting uneasy. It could be either one of them. Or maybe both. I'd figure it out.

No need to panic.

Not yet, anyway.

6

Soccer season should have been over by now, at least in this mother's opinion. The grass sparkled with frost in the morning light as the boys took the field. I found temperatures like this more suited to sledding or shoveling snow than sitting on the sidelines watching my son run around in shorts.

But he loved every minute of it. As far as he was concerned, any weather was good soccer weather. He would soon switch to indoor soccer, but he preferred to be outside. I think it was because he relished the feel of a cool rain on his face when he was running, the smell of the wet grass, and the way he could make clouds in the air with his breath and yet not feel cold.

I would have loved to spend my Saturday morning curled up with a good book and a cup of hot coffee. But instead I had cold coffee and a weekend with my kids. I told myself that their presence was really enough to keep me warm. Since they spent every other weekend with their father, my weekend time with them had become very precious.

That's what I told myself. In reality, I felt like I was wasting it. I should have spent quality time with my kids doing craft projects and science experiments. Instead, I yelled at them to pick up their junk and clean their rooms and turn down the TV while I did dishes and cleaned the bathrooms and waded through the stack of mail, newspapers, and other stuff that had piled up over the course of the week.

Evan's team won by one goal, and though he didn't score in this game, he had two assists and was enjoying the general euphoria of a team victory as we drove home. I was angry because I forgot to bring the clothes I needed to drop at the dry cleaners.

"You can drop them off when you take Alicia to her class," Evan suggested as he wolfed down a bag of mini-Oreos.

"Oh, rats. I forgot about drama." There was another big chunk out of the day. Her classes lasted an hour and a half and were at least twenty minutes away.

Evan looked at me like I'd grown an extra head. "How could you forget her class? She's been going since forever."

"I know." That made me even angrier. I should have factored that into the day. Now I had hardly any time to clean the house and mow the lawn. "Okay, when we get home, I want you to brush the dog and vacuum the living room."

"Me? Aww, why? You don't even let me plug in the vacuum cleaner by myself."

"You're old enough now. And don't worry—I'll assign Alicia some chores, too." I tried to calculate just when one of the kids would be big enough to push the lawn mower.

To Alicia, I assigned the task of sweeping and mopping the kitchen and bathroom floors. Then I went outside to mow, feeling as if I'd become a slave to the little green blades of grass. *Must keep them at the right height or the community association complains.* I wondered how they'd feel about artificial turf. Or I could take a big pile of dog hair, glue it down, and spray paint it green.

Since I'd bought a cheap mower, it was hard to push and hard to maneuver around the bushes and trees, and I was worn out and in an even worse mood than before when I shoved the mower into the shed and came back inside. At least I would only have to do this a few more times this season.

I took off my shoes on the back porch so I wouldn't track leaves and grass on the nice clean floors. A wasted effort as it turned out, because the floors were just as full of crumbs and dog hair as they'd been before I went out. Both kids lay sprawled on the couch, mouths open, eyes glazed as they watched some inane cartoon.

"Turn it off. Now!" I ordered. I was mad. Thirsty and mad. I'd been working my butt off while those two freeloaders sat drooling in front of the TV.

"I told you to vacuum in here," I yelled at Evan. Then I turned to Alicia. "And you were supposed to clean the kitchen floor."

"And the bathroom floors," Evan added.

"Don't talk to me about her chores when you haven't done your own," I snapped. "So why haven't you done what I asked?"

"I forgot," Evan mumbled.

"I was studying my lines." Alicia picked up a book, hurriedly opened it, and started mouthing words.

"Get busy, then," I called over my shoulder as I headed up the stairs. A flash of cellophane on a small bookshelf caught my eye and I turned around. "Who left this bag of chips out?" I asked.

No one answered.

"Who was eating chips in here?" I asked again, annoyance raising the volume of my voice without effort.

"Not me," Evan called up.

"I didn't," Alicia added.

I stomped into the bathroom and threw the bag in the trash. "Evan, you left the toilet seat up again." I fumed.

"I didn't do it," he insisted.

"Not believable. You're the only one who ever raises it."

"Well, I didn't leave it up."

"Go vacuum."

I wanted to cry. So this was my Saturday with the kids. The enriching weekend of time shared together with the two people I loved most in the whole world. All I could do was yell at them. But I felt like I couldn't trust them anymore. If they could so easily lie to me about chores, couldn't they lie about other things, too? Could I trust them not to steal or cheat in school? And what happened when we got to sex and drugs? I did cry at that thought, the sound muffled by the running water and the flushing of the toilet. It only took a minute to wash away deadly germs. Deadly uncertainty would hang on me like a noose.

Alicia appeared at the door with a mop and bucket. "Mom, are you almost done? I need to hurry up and get this room mopped or I'll be late for class."

I reached for the mop. "Let me do it. You get your stuff together. It won't take a minute and then we can go."

She offered a smile, not large, but enough to shrink the lump that had grown in my throat. "Are you upset because of *him*?"

I sniffed. "I'm not upset." Okay, wasn't I always telling them how important it was to be honest? And hadn't I begun to realize how often I was not? "Well," I reached for a tissue, "I'm not upset about. . .anything important."

"Are you sure? We, uh, noticed that he hasn't been here for a while."

"Do you miss him?"

She shook her head quickly. "Oh, *no*, no, don't worry about that." She looked suddenly very awkward. "I'll meet you downstairs."

What was that supposed to mean? I shoved the mop into the corner and water oozed into crevices where I'd never be able to wipe it up. She didn't like Brian? She had always acted like she did. She even went to volunteer at the historical site where he works on Saturdays, where she could dress up and play the role of a colonial indentured servant with melodramatic fervor.

So was she suggesting that Evan didn't miss having him around? Was it difficult for him to accept the sight of another man with his mother? His father was with another woman, and that didn't seem to bother him. But maybe it did and he just couldn't talk to me about it, and instead he talked to Alicia.

"Jeffrey, you rat," I muttered into the dirty water as the mop swirled in its depths. "Why did you do this to them?" If he had just honored his marriage vows, none of this would be happening.

I scrubbed at a blob of dried shampoo that had oozed over the edge of the tub. Well, even if Jeff hadn't left me, I'd still have to clean the bathrooms every week.

"Mom!" Alicia called.

And take Alicia to drama class.

Some of life went on the same regardless of whether Jeff and I were married or divorced. After five years, the kids seemed to have adjusted. They still did well at school, had friends and hobbies. They had adjusted better than I had, in fact. But now that I was starting to put together a life of my own, maybe it was getting difficult for them.

I carried the bucket of dirty water downstairs and over to the patio door so I could pour it out onto a bush I didn't like. Eventually, I hoped a weekly dose of disinfectant cleaner might do it in. As I carried the bucket back to put it away, the fragments of glass in the broken ornament hanging in the window sparkled in the sunlight.

Had Evan broken the cross because it came from Brian? Or was it an accident, but subconsciously, he was striking out against Brian?

No. I watch too much TV. Or read too many magazine articles in the dentist's office.

I'm sure it was just an accident.

An accident he had denied.

"C'mon, Evan," I called upstairs. "It's time to go."

He obediently trotted out of his room with a portable video game tucked under his arm and his soccer ball balanced on his head. "Hey, Mom, watch!" He tilted his head forward, bounced the ball off his knee, and trapped it under the opposite foot. Or rather, he tried to trap it. Instead, the ball squirted out from under his foot, across the landing, down the stairs, and into the kitchen.

I cringed, but it was all over and nothing had been broken.

This time.

"Try not to do that in the house, okay?" I kept my voice soft. No more yelling today. I gave Evan's shoulders a squeeze as we walked out to the van. "After class, would you guys like to go to a movie?"

At one time, I would have immediately expected an enthusiastic "Yes!" But now Alicia preferred to do things with her friends on weekends, and movies and dinners out didn't seem to be much of a treat even to Evan anymore. So I didn't hold much hope.

But to my surprise, both kids responded affirmatively to my suggestion.

We spent the rest of the afternoon arguing about which movie we were going to see.

~

There was a message from Brian on my cell phone when we got out of the movie. I decided to wait until we finished our overpriced brick-oven pizza and went home before I listened to his message.

His voice sounded strained, distracted, not as rich and friendly as I remembered. He simply asked me to call him back.

"So, um, how've you been?" I asked after we'd exchanged greetings.

"Good. I missed you at practice last night." His voice was soft, and gave a hint that he might have missed more than just my assistance as a script reader. But it was probably just acting.

"Who'd you have read all *my* lines?"

He chuckled. "Casey read lines for the kids who were

missing. And, um, that's why I was calling."

"Casey did a better job than me, and you want to make her assistant director?"

"Not hardly. You're a great actress. I love the way you read the lines. But, um, it's, well, I have a favor to ask."

Uh-oh.

"Ben, the one who's playing the airplane—"

"The moping model airplane?"

"Yeah, that's the one. Well, he doesn't want to be an airplane. He wants to be a velociraptor. So I, um, was wondering whether you, uh, thought you might be able to help make a dinosaur costume."

"You're having a velociraptor in your Christmas play?"

"Ben is the only one who's shown up for every rehearsal, so I'd kind of like to reward him."

The last thing in the world I wanted to add to my schedule was a project for a kid I hardly knew. I didn't know what to say, so I just didn't say anything.

"I know this is a lot to ask," Brian said hesitantly.

"It is. Especially over the phone." I lowered my voice. "Even my kids have noticed that you don't come over to see me anymore."

"I was just over there. . ."

"It's been weeks. I made chicken piccata and it was hardly burned at all."

"It was really good."

So why haven't you accepted any of my invitations since then? I was afraid to ask these questions aloud. I was afraid I might hear him struggle to come up with an answer, a polite way to say that he was tired of me already. "The only time I see you anymore seems to be at rehearsals," I said at last.

"This is a busy time," he said, a defensive edge creeping into his voice. "I have rehearsals twice a week, meetings usually on Tuesdays, basketball practice on Mondays—"

"Basketball?"

"They really needed another coach for the nine- and ten-year-olds."

"And you volunteered?"

"If I hadn't, those kids wouldn't have been able to play."

So his schedule would not get any better after this silly show was over.

"I'm not sure this is going to work," I said slowly, twisting the phone cord around my arm.

"I understand if you can't manage the costume. I know you're busy."

"I didn't mean the costume." I meant us, but I couldn't bring myself to say it. I hated sharing Brian with his entire church youth group, the church basketball league, the church committees he served on. . .I was starting to really resent his church.

There was an awkward pause. "It's hard to talk on the phone," he said at last. "But I'll see you at church tomorrow, right?"

"Maybe." I started to make up an excuse. "Evan was coughing pretty bad earlier, so he might be coming down with something." I think he had probably just swallowed too much greasy movie popcorn, but it *might* be an illness of some sort. And he *might* be sick in the morning.

I knew then with certainty that I wouldn't be there. If Brian wasn't going to make time for me, then I didn't have to make time for his church.

7

Hey, I missed you yesterday," Brian's voice sang out of the answering machine when I came home from work Monday. "Will you be able to make the rehearsal on Friday? Hope your day was good, or at least as good as a Monday can be. Keep the faith! And call me back when you get the chance."

I didn't want to explain my absence from church or my unwillingness to come to any more play rehearsals. So I didn't call him that night or the next day. On Wednesday, I called on my way to work, hoping I'd just get his answering machine.

"H'llo."

I winced at the sound of his rushed greeting. "Hi Brian, it's Karen."

"Well of course it's you. What's up?"

"I didn't expect to find you at home."

"I have a meeting out in this area at 9:30, so it didn't make any sense to go into the office. So, how's Evan feeling?"

"Fine. Why do you. . ." My words trailed off as I remembered that I had intimated that he would be too sick for church on Sunday. "He's much better."

"Good. And no one else got the bug?"

"No."

"So will I see you on Friday?"

I took a deep breath. "I don't think so. Too much going on that night."

"Oh." He sounded more disappointed than I expected. Which was good as long as it was disappointment that he wouldn't see me and not disappointment that he was missing his director's assistant.

"Can you meet me for dinner on Saturday?" I asked quickly. The kids would be at their dad's this weekend, so I had time for Brian, if he had time for me.

"Sure." His voice brightened. "We can go over the director's notes."

"Oh, great."

"Where do you want to meet?"

"How about Cacao Lane?" Not as expensive as Tersiguel's but quite a bit more than the rehearsal-night pizzas. Since he always refused my offers to go Dutch, I guess I was testing him to see if he was at least willing to spend real money on me.

"I'll make a reservation for seven o'clock."

Okay, he passed that test. "See you then." I tried to put a smile in my voice and I thought maybe he did the same as he said good-bye.

When I reached the Blue Moon that morning, I was determined to keep my eyes on Eric as much as possible. He was the most likely candidate to be damaging merchandise. I figured he was probably working with someone to resell the damaged merchandise, so I needed to determine the partner's identity. The surly guy didn't seem like the type to confess, even if confronted with proof of his guilt. But his partner might.

He might be working with Carl, but if so, I'd bet Eric was the one doing the damaging and repairing. One of Carl's coworkers had confirmed that he had been virtually living at the firehouse for the last several weeks, taking extra shifts for others and volunteering to stay at the house on call even when he wasn't working.

So maybe Carl was helping to sell the damaged merchandise to get some extra money to get out of some kind of trouble.

The door to the Blue Moon was locked when I arrived and no one answered my knock. When I leaned against the glass and peered inside, I could see a big, dark armoire. With moving legs. It soon became apparent that the legs belonged to Eric. I knocked to get his attention, but he turned away and started toward the back of the store as if pretending he hadn't seen me.

I should have known better than to think he might be helpful, even for a moment.

What was more important than his rudeness, however, was the fact that he was there at all. That meant he had keys and access to the merchandise when others were not around.

Evidence of means and opportunity. Once I could ascribe a good motive. . .

Rather than wait out in the cold, I was just about to head out for a cup of coffee when I heard the jingle of keys behind me.

"Sorry I'm late," Vicki chimed.

I glanced at my watch. "I don't think you're late. I'm probably early."

She quickly flipped through the ring of keys until she

reached the right one, inserted it in the lock, and opened the door.

"Is there an alarm or something you need to shut off?" I asked.

"Yes, but if it was on, you'd hear a beep. And we don't, so that means Eric must have already come in and shut it off."

So Eric not only had a key, but he knew the alarm code.

My day was getting better and better.

When Eric lumbered by with a hand truck a few minutes later, I flashed him a big smile. He was making this case easier for me all the time.

Of course he did not return the smile. In fact, he ran over my foot with the hand truck. Fortunately, it was empty at the time or he might have broken half my toes. I didn't mind the blunder, because the more obnoxious he became, the more I wanted to see him put away. This would be much easier than my first case, where most of the suspects were so friendly that I didn't want to find anyone guilty.

Actually, there had been one guy who was almost as surly as Eric. He turned out to be innocent.

But I had never really suspected him to begin with. I had a gut feeling someone else had stolen the artifact that was missing from the museum's collection. This time, I had a gut feeling that my vandal was right in front of me, mowing down dust bunnies with a hand truck.

I wondered if employees like me were responsible for dusting the floors. They sure needed it. And dusting would give me an excuse to look at things from odd angles.

Vicki was hurrying down the next aisle with a painting clutched to her chest. I waved to get her attention. "Hey, is it okay if I dust some?"

She blinked in surprise. "Oh, yeah, if you think it needs it. We have lint-free cloths to use on the glass, and with the oil paintings, you dust only the frame, of course. You don't want to touch the canvas. We have special blowers for that."

"I was thinking about the floors, actually." The paintings on the walls, as far as I could tell, looked great. But on the floor, great globs of dust rolled by like tumbleweeds under the tables and other furniture every time I walked by. "Is there a dust mop in the back?"

She grimaced as if I'd suggested using my cardigan to clean the men's bathroom. "That's a job for the porter."

"Well, he seems busy, and I'm not at the moment."

She shrugged. "You can check, then." She hurried away, with the unique poised walk that reminded me of flight attendants cruising through an airline terminal. I glanced at the painting in her arms to see if it was the same as the one she'd moved before, but the colors looked too bright.

Vicki was obviously very into art.

While she engaged in the hunt for optimum lighting, I headed back to look for a dust mop. The junky repair room at the back seemed to have everything but cleaning implements. Every flat surface was littered with clamps of every shape and size, glue, sealant, caulk, and more colors of paint than a preschool. I briefly considered trying to dust with a paint roller.

"Need something?" Eric asked.

His voice made me jump. I hadn't seen him crouched down on the floor, prying broken tiles off a fireplace mantel that looked very lonely without a fire or a place.

"I need to find a dust mop." But actually, I wanted to watch him work, if I could. I surmised that he learned to make repairs here at the Blue Moon, then devised a scheme to secretly damage their merchandise, have a partner buy it at a reduced rate, and sell it elsewhere for much more, splitting the profits.

Of course, I couldn't watch him work at the moment, because he wasn't working. He was watching me. He nodded in my direction. "Behind the door."

"Thank you." A direct and timely answer. That was unexpectedly helpful.

I started forward to look behind the door but stopped when I realized he was speaking to me again.

"I, uh. . ." He cleared his throat and looked down at his hands. "I want to apologize for not letting you in earlier. I didn't know you worked here. I—I mean I didn't realize it was you."

Eric was apologizing to me? I grabbed the doorknob to steady myself. "That's okay. Vicki let me in."

A shy smile crept over his face and I realized he looked completely transformed, like the before and after picture on an ad for exercise equipment. He seemed taller even. "Vicki's nice like that." He paused, as if searching for a stronger word. "Real nice," he said at last.

The way I saw it, Vicki was paid to let me in. But, hey, if Eric saw it as extra nice behavior, so be it. "Well, so anyway, like I said. It's okay."

His attention went back to his crowbar, so I turned

to the dust mop, which looked as if it were made *of* dust rather than for it. This explained the state of the floors.

When I shook out some of the dust over a trash can, the whole mop head came off, too. I wondered if they might do better setting the thing out for sale as a source of antique dust rather than actually trying to dust with it.

"Do you sell a lot of Tollefsen paintings or other paintings at the auctions?" I asked Eric as I tried to screw the loose head of the dust mop back on.

"We sell a lot of artwork, but it's whatever the consignor puts in. Haven't noticed a lot of Tollefsens. Mostly prints."

Again, he was unexpectedly civil and informative. Had he decided he liked me now? Or was this not Eric but a non-evil twin? I couldn't help but test him a little. I loomed over him, blocking the light from the overhead bulbs. "What are you working on?" When my kids do this to me, it drives me crazy.

But it didn't seem to set him off. "I'm trying to replace some of the broken tiles on this mantel," he answered, not looking up from his work. "I noticed there were some extras taped to the back." He rubbed his nose with the side of his hand. "They must have been attached to the wall itself or part of the mantel that stayed behind. So if I scrape the mortar off, I can use them to replace a few of the broken ones."

"That sounds like a lot of work."

He shrugged. "I'm not too busy today."

I decided I had blocked his light for long enough. "Well, I'm off to dust. See you."

He nodded.

I contemplated this unexpected change as I pushed

the dusty mop around the even dustier dull floorboards. He had a real guilty look about him when he apologized for not letting me in, so I decided that maybe he wasn't a bad person, it was just that he was in a bad mood when I'd seen him before. And when he wasn't in a bad mood, he felt guilty for the moods. I contemplated buying him a mood ring, just to give all the rest of us warning.

As I pushed a herd of dust bunnies under the end pieces of a sleigh bed, I bent down to look for damage. A big gouging scratch out of the dark wood would surely reduce the price, and yet Eric could probably cover it over later. But the bed looked fine. I let my gaze travel to the piece next to it, a spindly coatrack made of powder-coated iron. Not attractive, but better than the antlers we used at the office. Maybe we could arrange to take some of our fees in merchandise.

Above the coatrack was a painting of cherubs frolicking in fluffy white clouds, like toddlers in a ball pit at Chuck E. Cheese's. I hadn't examined any of the paintings for damage. There might have been some that Mr. and Mrs. P. hadn't noticed.

The cherubs had piercing blue eyes, rosy red cheeks, and almost fluorescent white teeth. After a moment, I wanted to damage that painting myself. I decided to look for some more pictures of dead things.

As I examined everything on the long east wall of the gallery, I found no more damage and not even any paintings that I felt needed damaging. The phone rang several times, but Vicki always got to it before me, and most of the calls concerned the whereabouts of the appraiser, Sarah, who worked for a variety of different galleries. If people liked the appraisals she wrote on behalf of the Blue Moon, they were more likely to engage the gallery to auction their estate goods for them. Since none of the damage had occurred to auction merchandise, though, I figured I could ignore her. Her records had turned up nothing out of the ordinary.

"I think I might like to be an appraiser someday," Vicki mused after she hung up the phone the last time. "Sarah's taking a potential estate auction to lunch at Tersiguel's."

"She's taking an auction to lunch?"

"I mean someone who might auction their estate through us."

"It must be a pretty impressive estate." Tersiguel's was a restaurant in a white clapboard house that looked as if it had been transported directly from a small town in France. I couldn't even afford to look at the menu in the window, let alone order anything from it. I would have needed a second mortgage to get past the soup course.

Vicki sighed with a longing look toward the front door. "I love their *socca niçoise*."

"Well, maybe Sarah will bring you some." Of whatever it was.

She laughed. "Maybe."

But instead it was Mrs. Photopoulos who came in with a treat, some cranberry scones from the Old Mill Bakery. When the weather gets cold, I just want to eat and eat. And fresh, hot scones beat the living daylights out of the waxy chocolate donuts we always seem to have around the office. We stood around the counter eating, spraying crumbs all over the glass with each bite.

"Not too busy today, eh?" Mrs. P. asked between mouthfuls.

I shook my head and caught a glimpse of something out of the corner of my eye.

"We gave directions to a woman earlier," Vicki said. "So we might see her."

I shook my head again.

"Why? Don't you think she'll come in?"

I wasn't shaking my head to say no, I was shaking my head to see what it was that had caught my eye a moment ago.

"Oh, no." Mrs. P. set her scone down on the counter.

A sinking feeling weighted my chest. Another painting was damaged. I could see why I hadn't noticed at first. The rip was small, only about an inch or so in the blue sky background of a painting of Ellicott City back before it was called "city," and probably before the Ellicotts had moved there.

"Another Tollefsen!" Mrs. P. cried in an anguished voice.

I was surprised; the quaint historical landscape picture was quite different from the dark, surreal paintings I had so far seen ascribed to Tollefsen. "That's one of his?" I pointed to the picture of rolling hills overlooking the river.

"No, up there." She pointed to the painting just above it. It was the shadowy image that might have been a man's garish face, but it would have been a dead man, because there was a four inch cut severing the head from where a neck would be had the artist felt the need to include one. If Mrs. P. hadn't pointed it out, I might have assumed the cut was part of the gruesome image, painted in and not actually cut into the canvas. The painting was up so high on the wall, it was hard to tell unless you knew, as we all did now, that we were looking for an actual cut in the canvas.

"I can't believe it!" Mrs. P. glared at me.

I stared back up at the wall. "I can't either." She hadn't noticed the damage to the other painting, or maybe she noticed and didn't care because it wasn't worth as much as the Tollefsen.

"I thought it was your job to protect us from—"

"Yes," I cut in quickly before she could say something that would totally blow my cover. "On quiet days like this, our most important job as employees is to keep watch over the store. And somehow we let this happen."

The store owner slowly advanced toward me shaking with rage. "I should fire you right now."

"No, Mrs. P," Vicki said in a horror-stricken voice. "I'm sure this happened when Karen wasn't here. It must have happened while the store was closed."

"I don't care." Mrs. P.'s fiery stare would have burned a hole through me if I had stood still long enough. Her voice came out in a low growl. "I should have Mr. P. fire you."

"But it's not Karen's fault," Vicki insisted, clutching Mrs. P.'s arm.

"I'm sure," I explained to Vicki, hoping desperately to retain the illusion that I was just another store clerk, "Mrs. Photopoulos thought hiring an additional employee would make the premises more secure."

Mrs. P. nodded. "Yes. Exactly."

I was saved from immediate dismissal by the sound of the proverbial bell. The door jangled to let us know someone had arrived. "Mr. P. will want to talk with you when he gets back," Mrs. P. spat out before she spun away and stalked toward her office.

"Hey, Vicki," a tall, elegant Asian woman called from

the doorway. "How're you guys doing today?" She raised her voice as she noticed Mrs. P. in the back of the store. "Hello, Mrs. Photopoulos."

Mrs. P. grunted in response, but didn't even turn around.

"Don't mind her, Sarah." Vicki waved dismissively. "She's just in one of her moods."

Well, she had reason to be, but I saw no need to explain that.

"This is Karen," Vicki continued in her usual friendly voice, waving toward me. "She's new. Karen, this is Sarah Kuo, our appraiser."

I nodded. "Nice to meet you,"

"And you." Sarah's high-heeled leather mules clicked against the floorboards as she walked toward us. "I think you'll like working here; the Blue Moon attracts some of the best clientele in the area."

"Even though our porter is the biggest troll and he won't leave me alone," Vicki added with a giggle. "Why can't we have one of those phat guys that work down at Caplan's?"

"You want to work with fat guys?" I asked.

She giggled again. "*P–H–A–T*: pretty hot and tempting. Not the other kind."

"I have to agree with you about Eric," Sarah said as she turned toward the scheduling book by the phone. "And Carl's almost as bad." She flipped through the pages. "None of my afternoon appointments are coming in here, right? I think I'm out on New Cut Road and then over in Dickeyville."

"That sounds right." Vicki traced a line of entries down the page. "Yep. 1:30."

Sarah smiled. "I'd better get going then. But I couldn't resist stopping in since I was so close."

"How was lunch?"

"I don't know if we've got the estate; they're talking to one other place tomorrow."

"No, I mean the food. I love Tersiguel's." Vicki cast a longing glance toward the street.

"Good as usual. Today I tried this frog leg appetizer that really—"

"You ate frog legs!" Turning back to Sarah with a look of outraged disgust, Vicki slammed the schedule book on the counter.

Sarah started to back toward the door. "Yeah, well, I'm sorry but—"

"I can't believe you ate the legs of innocent frogs!" Vicki's voice rose to a furious squeal.

I was tempted to ask why that was worse than eating the legs of innocent chickens, but the change in Vicki's demeanor really concerned me. She didn't just look or sound upset, she *was* upset. Her hands were shaking and her eyes looked like they might pop from excess pressure. Tears began to rush down her cheeks in a torrent.

"It's okay," I said gently, glancing at Sarah to see how she responded to Vicki's sudden explosion.

Sarah just rolled her eyes. "I'll check in when I hear about the Eldwin estate." She waved and hurried toward the door.

"Killer!" Vicki screamed after her.

I was really glad we had no customers.

When the door jangled closed, Vicki sagged back against the counter. "Oh, those poor innocent frogs."

I remembered now that Vicki had frogs on her car somewhere. And there was that ugly frog statue she'd talked to. She must have a thing about frogs.

"Are you okay, Vicki?" Mrs. P. shuffled out of the office toward us at twice her usual speed.

"Y—yes," she sniffed. "But I'm never speaking to Sarah again."

Mrs. P. shook her head. "I thought someone had been killed, the way you screamed."

"Someone *was* killed. Many someones."

Mrs. P. looked around. "But not here, right?"

"No. At Tersiguel's."

"Okay." Mrs. P. patted her hand. "Try not to get so upset when you're working, all right? It can scare the customers. It scares me. Now you." She turned to me and her expression went from one meant to be comforting to one that would no doubt leave me in need of comfort later. "Come to the office. Mr. P. wants to talk to you."

The walk to the back of the store seemed to take about three times as long as it had earlier in the day. They were going to fire me. This would be my last case, and then I'd be stuck typing invoices for the rest of my life.

Ahead of me, Mrs. P. chugged toward the office like a steam locomotive.

Mr. P. looked up from a set of account books when he heard us come in. "Was Vicki upset about the painting?"

"Nah." Mrs. P. shook her head. "She's angry with Sarah about something. You know how she gets sometimes."

Did Vicki fly into tantrums of rage like this on other topics, or just frog legs?

Mr. P. nodded as he turned toward me. "We have a

problem with you, Mrs. Maxwell."

"I'm sorry about the painting," I said quickly. I had warned them they would not be getting a security guard, but decided reminding them would not make them feel any better.

"We hired you because we heard you did such a great job for the historical society. But you've let us down."

"I am sorry. It takes time to build a case." And now DS Investigations would probably be fired from the case, because I had to make a further confession.

I took a deep breath. "That Tollefsen painting is not the only new damage."

"What?" Mr. and Mrs. P. rumbled in unison.

"The picture below it on the wall, the landscape. It has a cut in it, too."

"Why?" Mrs. P. moaned as she leaned back against a shelf full of broken china figurines.

Chair legs squeaked against the floorboards as Mr. P. pushed back away from his desk. "Let me see."

I led him out to the site of the latest damage. Then I took another deep breath. "You may want to reconsider reporting this to your insurer. The loss may be enough now to offset the increase in premiums."

He shook his head, still staring up at the damaged paintings. "After they pay the claim, our company will cancel us completely. And no one else would give us coverage, at least not until we have someone behind bars for this."

"This should be enough to make the police take notice."

His lips curled into a humorless smile. "Yeah. They can't possibly tell us it was an accident this time."

"You couldn't accidentally damage a painting up that high."

I looked around to see if anyone else could overhear us. Vicki was on the phone at the front of the store and I could hear Eric hammering on something in the back.

I prepared to talk us right out of the job. It wouldn't make Dave real happy, but at this point, the clients might need to explore their other options. "So what you probably need to do," I said in a low voice, "is get the police to come out and then hire a uniformed security service to keep watch when the store is closed. They'll provide surveillance at a cheaper rate than a full-service investigation firm like ours."

Mr. P. frowned. "I can't afford surveillance. And I need investigation, too. I wanna find out who did this to us."

"The police generally investigate crimes, don't they?"

He scratched the back of his head. "I don't know that they do so well with that. We had someone break into our apartment when we were first married. They took everything we had and we got none of it back. Police never found anything."

"They might this time."

"They might. But I want you to keep working on it, at least for another week or so. I'll stay here at night with my dog—he'll keep anyone out, I can guarantee that—and we'll see if you find out anything. The neighbors say you did a great job working for the historical society."

Elation shot through my veins as I thanked Mr. P. I had a week's reprieve!

The Blue Moon had hired *me*, specifically me, not Dave but me, because they heard I was good.

And Dave hadn't told me. He let me think he was doing me a favor giving me the case.

But I couldn't dwell on that now. For the rest of today, I needed to gather as much evidence against Eric as I could.

As if he realized I was watching, he behaved like a model employee, polishing lamp bases, tightening loose hinges on every cabinet door in the store, and repeatedly asking Vicki if she needed him to run down to the store to buy more tissues.

Either I was completely wrong about his personality, or I was completely right about his guilt. And he was starting to feel extremely guilty.

8

The next morning when I stepped inside our office building, I noticed that the old light fixture over the stairs had been replaced by something that looked like it had been pulled off the *Titanic*. But at least we had light again, which was some progress. I ran back downstairs, opened the door, and peered up at the front of the building.

The shutter was hanging straight next to the window as I had always assumed it was. Had I only imagined that it was broken, or had Rodney the office maximizer already convinced the landlord to fix it?

I hurried back upstairs to see what else had changed in my absence. Just as I had expected, the door was unlocked, which was potentially very dangerous. I could be the disgruntled wife of a client coming to take revenge against the agency for ruining my marriage.

I yanked the door open, ready to berate somebody for following Rodney's stupid advice. But the words died in my throat when I saw the place. For starters, I couldn't see anyone to berate. A wall of potted palms stood where my desk used to be, and I had to step around the greenery before I could see much of anything else. In the corner where Dave's desk had been before he moved into his old partner's office, there now stood a modular cubicle with a Formstone rock fountain in front of it. As if mildew wasn't enough of a problem in the damp old place.

The door to Dave's office was closed. And it had a

wreath of eucalyptus leaves hanging on it. The kitchen was now screened by a beaded curtain, and I didn't even want to guess what Rodney had done to the bathroom. File cabinets which had been spaced strategically throughout the office now stood in a single row in the back next to the copier. Brittany's computer desk had been replaced with a rolltop desk, covered and apparently locked. My desk was nowhere to be seen.

"Dave?"

The only answer was the sound of gurgling water from that fountain and some synthesized new age music. I walked over to unplug the fountain.

"Hey!" Rodney protested from somewhere inside the cubicle.

I peered around the edge and found him with head-phones on his ears sitting in front of a new flat-panel computer monitor that was about three feet wide. Words danced around on the screen as if he were a contestant in a game show. He jumped to his feet, hampered slightly by the headphone cords. "Mrs. Maxwell, what do you think you're doing?"

I nodded toward the screen. "I was going to ask you the same thing."

"This program is configuring possibilities for my new filing system."

"What new filing system?"

A smug grin spread across his face. "The filing system that will take this office to the next level."

"The old filing system is just fine." I crossed my arms in front of my chest.

"It was just fine for the old business. But for the

maximized business we will need a maximized filing system."

"We have a fully functional filing system based on twenty-six un-maximized letters of the alphabet. Perhaps you've heard of them?"

His grin grew even more smug. "It is just that kind of small-minded thinking that kept this business from growing as it should."

"What do you mean?"

"I mean that until I arrived, this business operated like a family grocery store."

He had a point. As much as I tried to keep organized logs, client information files, and regular reports, Dave had a way of sabotaging me. Even at the conclusion of his most successful cases, I always had to scramble to reconstruct what he'd done so we could bill the client for it.

"Not even a grocery," he sniffed. "A lemonade stand."

That made me angry. Yes, we were a little casual with our records. But now he'd gone too far.

"We have been a very successful business without your help," I pointed out. "Last quarter we grossed over $70,000."

He leaned over with a smile. "Yesterday, I prepared a contract for regular surveillance and background work with Consolidated Building Maintenance. Using contract investigators, we will be able to bill out $70,000 *every month*."

I felt another rush of air, which meant my mouth was hanging open again. In the few days he'd been here, Rodney had added more business than we'd acquired in the entire first half of the year. I'd never heard of Consolidated

Building—if Dave had been courting them, he would have told me. At the very least, I would have paid bills for lunches with some decision-maker who liked to eat at places like Tersiguel's. Could Rodney have done this entirely on his own?

I looked around in disbelief. I had been replaced by someone capable of thinking on a much bigger scale. Daring to approach big clients. Daring to rearrange the office.

Daring to move my stuff without asking. "Where's my desk?" I asked finally.

He nodded toward the closet. "I believe you said you preferred to work in there."

Oh, great. So this joker couldn't recognize sarcasm when he heard it? I headed over to see whether he'd really managed to move my desk and cabinets into the narrow space.

The electrician who put the *Titanic* light in our stairwell had put a similar device in the closet, or I should say, my new private office. My new private, electrically lit shoebox. There was room for my desk but not really room to sit down at it. I looked around. "Where's my chair?"

"It didn't fit." Rodney gestured toward a strange low-cushioned contraption on wheels. "I ordered an ergonomic secretary's chair for you. It fits the space, it reflects the new proactive tone we seek to project, and it will help correct your posture defects, ultimately saving the company on medical expenses."

"I'm not a secretary," I muttered as I stared around in disbelief. "What kind of chair did you buy to correct Dave's defects?" I asked. "Or your own?"

He threw back his head in a really phony laugh. "Ha,

ha, a sense of humor is so important in maintaining an upbeat office rapport."

I was starting to think that perhaps it wouldn't be so bad to be isolated in a closet after all. Glancing at the answering machine, I saw no new messages, which meant that Brian hadn't called. He hadn't called me at home, either.

"Well, I'd better get back to my files." He meant his computer game.

As he started back toward his cubicle, I tried to remember what else I'd needed to say to him. Something about the files reminded me. What was the problem? Beside the fact that we'd probably never find anything once he'd refiled everything according to the phases of the moon or whatever he was using.

His shoes squeaked on what appeared to be a freshly waxed floor.

"Rodney!" I yelped, suddenly remembering the problem.

"Mr. Cadle."

I waved aside his objection. "Whatever. We have a problem."

His eyebrows arched as if to say he considered *me* the problem.

"You moved the file cabinets."

"Yes. They are now located for maximum efficiency."

"You can't move the file cabinets."

"Their placement before made no sense whatsoever. It was terribly inefficient."

"It made perfect sense. The cabinets were arranged to avoid the termite damage in the floorboards."

"Should I call the exterminator?"

"We don't have termites now. It was old damage."

"Well then, there's no need to worry."

"The damage is still there. The floor is weak in several places. And the weight of the heavy cabinets will make it worse. One day they could crash right through to the office below." I smacked my hands together for emphasis. "Just like that."

He let out another phony laugh that was so annoying I thought it might actually be genuine. "That's impossible."

"It's not. The termite inspector told me one time about a house in Catonsville where—"

He held up his hand. "A house. A *house*, you said. Well, the building codes are much more stringent for business property."

"I'll bet they weren't in the 1800s when this building was built."

"The landlord would not rent this property if it were unsafe for the purpose for which it was intended."

"You don't know our landlord."

"Well," he dusted his hands together in a dismissive gesture, "the arrangement of the office is my job now, so if we have a little—" He gave that laugh again. "—*crash*, then I will take full responsibility."

"Fine." I gave up and raked my hand through my hair. "Where's Dave?"

"Mr. Sarkesian."

"Where's *my brother*?"

Rodney's complacent smile faltered a little. "H–he's in his office. Organizing."

Organizing? Right. If he was actually here this early, Dave would be eating donuts and shooting wadded-up napkins at the basketball hoop I recently attached to his trash can.

"I'll go help him."

"He said he needs to work alone."

"I'm his sister. He'll ignore me and it'll be like I'm not even there." As I headed back to tell Dave about the progress at the Blue Moon, I kept reminding myself that this was what I wanted, someone else to handle the office work so I could focus more on investigation. I just hadn't expected the office to fall apart quite so quickly.

"What do you mean you told me?" I glared at the phone receiver, as if I could somehow visually transmit the disgust I felt for my ex-husband at that moment.

Jeff's voice took on a whiny nasal tone. "Last time I said I would have to drop them off early this weekend."

"I thought you meant 7:00 Sunday night instead of 8:00. Instead you're dropping them off at 7:00 on *Saturday*."

"What's the big deal?"

"I have plans tonight." And I wasn't comfortable leaving the kids alone at night.

"Plans?" He seemed surprised. "So take the kids along."

"No," I said firmly. Brian and I needed time alone. Having Evan and Alicia along would be just as bad as a roomful of crabby candy canes.

Well, not quite as bad. And I did miss them when they were with Jeff. "Bring the kids home at 9:00," I allowed. "I'll arrange to be home by then."

His nasal tone turned to a sneer. "They didn't want to come home early, anyway."

"Yes, I'm aware they prefer life in LindaLand. Anything else obnoxious you want to say before I hang up on you? No? Good. Bye." I slammed the phone into the cradle with far more force than was necessary.

Well, maybe it was necessary for my state of mind, if not the phone itself. Why did that man have the ability to make me so dysfunctional? Here I'd been contentedly getting ready for my date with Brian—well, so far all I'd done was try on and discard blouses, but at least I wasn't *mad* at any of them.

Of course, I wasn't exactly contented, either. I was worried. What was I going to say to Brian about not wanting to go to church or to play practices? I couldn't say anything about him not taking me out to dinner because he *was* taking me out to dinner. But something was wrong between us and I didn't know what to say about it or if I should say anything at all. Maybe all relationships went like this and I just didn't know better.

I heard Brian's truck pull up while I was still deciding which shoes to wear. Grabbing a pair of low-heeled boots, I ran downstairs to shove the dog in the backyard before she could set off on a round of mad barking. I didn't arrive in time to prevent the vicious noise, but at least I got to her before she launched herself at the window on the door. People tell me it's unnerving to see rows of teeth snapping at them from behind the chiffon curtains.

"Are you ready?" Brian asked as I opened the door. "I think I'm running a few minutes late."

And we had to be back earlier than planned, too. So

we didn't have any time to waste. I sat down on the stairs to pull on my boots, hoping I wasn't getting dog hair all over my long skirt.

Brian reached down to help me up. I had a sudden memory of him doing the same thing when we first met. His hands were just as warm and strong now as they had been then, and I suddenly wished I had the chance to feel that warmth more often.

He let go of my hand to open the door.

Neither of us said much on the way to the restaurant. Out the window I watched the parade of Christmas lights that people somehow found time to put up. Everything from simple white candles to garish collections of giant blow-up toys bobbing on tether lines. When we reached Main Street, I was surprised to see so many people walking up and down the sidewalks. Many carried cups of steaming beverages and strolled and laughed as if they were in no particular hurry to get anywhere.

"Moonlight Madness," Brian murmured as he looked in vain for a place to park.

"Christmas shoppers or werewolves?" I asked as I marveled at all the people.

He grinned. "Shoppers most likely. But they can be as dangerous as wolves if you pick up something they want to buy." He stopped and put the truck in neutral. "I'll let you out at the restaurant to hold our reservation. It may take me awhile to find a parking space."

I nodded, feeling the clock ticking as I opened the door and slid down to the pavement. It was seven now. We had to be home at nine. It might take him half an hour to park and walk to the restaurant. . . .

By the time I'd finished the calculations, I was already inside the dark, cozy establishment, where candlelit tables nestled against the stone walls and wooden beams crossed low overhead. Would Brian have to stoop to keep from hitting his head? He was so much taller than Jeff.

Not that Jeff had taken me here very often.

A young hostess offered to show me to our table, but I decided to wait for Brian by the door. I read the specials board so many times that I'd almost started composing a tune to go along with the list of salmon *beurre blanc* and pork medallions with toasted onion potatoes.

No frog legs. I wondered whether Vicki would throw a fit if she thought I'd been in a restaurant that served them. I glanced up the street to see if I could see the Blue Moon, but the street curved just enough to block the view.

Since I was thinking of the Blue Moon, I started to consider ways to confront Eric, when the time was right. If he was feeling guilty, which certainly seemed to be the case, I could use that to my advantage.

A warm hand rested on my shoulder. "I thought I was far away, but I think you're even farther."

I smiled at the sound of Brian's rich, low voice. "I didn't hear you come in."

"Obviously." He glanced at the board quickly as the hostess beckoned us toward the back of the room. "Any good specials?"

"Uh, I can't remember." What kind of a lousy investigator was I anyway? I had a thirty-second memory.

We followed the hostess up a flight of steep stairs into another room with a fireplace at one end. She led us to a table close enough so that I could see the flames dancing over Brian's shoulder when we sat down.

"This is even nicer than I'd remembered."

He looked at his watch. "Uh, yeah. I've always liked this place." Though he looked around for a moment, his gaze soon returned to his watch.

"Do you have somewhere to go after this?" The watch thing was starting to get a little annoying. I made time for his hobbies, and now when I wanted to do something, he made me feel like I was wasting his precious time.

"No, I just have some stuff to finish up for Sunday School tomorrow."

I sat back and crossed my arms in front of my chest. "Oh, so you were able to schedule me in between volunteering at the 1776 House and preparing for Sunday School?"

He shrugged. "It was your idea."

"So I'm just another item on the agenda."

"No, no, of course not." The accusing tone in my voice was starting to make him defensive in return. "But time is tight, and I guess I'm pretty used to keeping close track of it."

I leaned forward. "When was the last time you did something that wasn't planned or scheduled? Something spontaneous?"

He gaped for a moment. "I don't know. This, I guess. I don't usually go out to dinner on Saturday nights."

"We planned this days ago. That's not spontaneous. Think of something else."

"I, uh, parked on the left side of the street a few minutes ago. I don't normally do that."

"A slight aberration in parking habits was not what I

had in mind. You need to stop living by that rigid schedule of yours. Skip a meeting and go to a movie instead. Stop and look in the windows of the stores on Main Street." I wanted to say *bring me flowers* or *call me just because you want to talk*. But I didn't.

He shook his head. "You don't understand. I have responsibilities."

"We all have responsibilities. But life should be more than one giant 'to do' list."

"Hi," a cheerful young woman's voice chirped from over my shoulder. "I'm Brandi, and I'll be your server this evening. Would you like to hear the specials?"

"Yes." Brian smiled at her. Not at me. But then, why should he smile at me? I'd just spent the last several minutes treating him like a hostile witness in a murder trial. While the waitress recited the descriptions of the salmon, pork, and other specials I thought I'd memorized earlier, I considered what I'd been saying, and my bossy tone of voice. And I reminded myself that I had to cut it out before Brian got fed up with me.

I ordered a chicken dish I remembered from the last time I was there, and Brian ordered a steak. The smile stayed on his face even after the waitress scurried away to place our order.

"So, what were we talking about?"

"Nothing," I muttered, looking down at the napkin I had forgotten to put in my lap.

"Oh, no, it was definitely something."

"No, nothing important." If he couldn't remember, all the better. We'd just let the matter drop.

He gave up and looked around the room, as if he

hoped to join in the conversation at another table.

I was boring him.

"Those must be the garlic mashed potatoes." He waved toward a plate on a tray nearby. "They look good. Wish I'd ordered those."

I looked at the potatoes. He was probably thinking he was glad I hadn't cooked dinner.

"I think I picked a baked potato," he continued when I said nothing. "What did you get with yours?"

"I don't remember."

We were silent again, and the laughter and conversation of diners at the other tables seemed to underscore the lack of any at our own.

"Oh, before I forget," Brian said, his face brightening, "Patty and Paula said to say 'hi.' They asked if you might come back to visit the 1776 House some Saturday."

"Yeah." I wished I could muster more enthusiasm. "That'd be fun. I think Alicia misses it a little."

"Hey, you should come for the Christmas workshop. We have extra visitors and I could use Evan's help in the blacksmith shop."

I could almost see Brian making notes in a calendar.

"December's a busy month," was all I said.

I almost said what I was thinking, that I was tired of being his assistant, or scheduling my kids to be his assistants. But I didn't want to seem angry anymore, even if I still was. So instead, I watched a drop of condensation on my water glass as it trickled unevenly along the prints my fingers had left on the glass.

Brian looked at his watch again. "Slow service tonight."

I nodded, still not trusting myself to speak in a conversational manner.

"I think the play's coming along real well."

That was not a topic likely to produce pleasant conversation. So I said nothing.

He looked at the other tables, again leaving me with the impression that I was boring him.

I couldn't think of anything to say.

Fortunately, our food arrived soon after, and we could discuss that for a few minutes.

We ate.

"Would either of you care for dessert or coffee?" our pert waitress said hopefully when we'd finished.

Brian looked at me.

I shook my head. "I have to get back. Jeff's dropping the kids off at 9:00."

"Oh, so that's why you've been so tense. You should have said something." He grinned. "We could have gone to McDonalds for faster service."

I started to make a joke about him trying to get out of spending money on me, but then I thought he might take it seriously and get offended. So I just offered a lame smile.

He seemed very far away in the cab of his pickup truck as we drove home. When we pulled up outside the house, I just sat and looked at him for a moment, wishing he could read my mind and know that I wanted him to like me, to find me interesting, but I just wasn't sure what to say to him anymore.

I wanted him to kiss me goodnight.

He put the truck in park and reached over to give my hand a squeeze. "Take care, okay? Keep the faith."

"You usually only say that on the phone." Maybe that

was a sign of how distant we'd been tonight.

"Do I?" He pulled out his cell phone. "I can pretend if you'd like."

"No." I squeezed his hand in return. "This is better than the phone." Or seeing him at a rehearsal, or volunteering at the blacksmith shop.

He leaned across, close enough to graze my cheek with a kiss. "I'm glad you think so." His voice was low, soft, almost a whisper, and I wasn't sure if I'd imagined the kiss.

Before I could respond, he'd pulled away again. Neither of us said anything about when we'd see each other next.

9

After we said our good-byes, I made my trek through the cold darkness up to the house, where the dog howled and threw herself viciously at the door as if I had come to steal the family stash of rawhide treats. "You can't bark like that at me," I insisted as I unlocked the door. "I'm the one who buys your dog food."

She jumped up, demanding love and affection, but giving as much as she got. At least I always knew where I stood with Tara. If she wanted something, she'd come up and bark. If she got bored with me, she'd leave. And if I got mad and lost my temper, she'd cringe for a moment and forget all about it the next. Maybe what I needed in my life was not a boyfriend but just a better behaved dog.

In the distance, I could hear Brian's truck turn the corner. I put my hand to my cheek where he'd kissed me, like a schoolgirl with a crush. He was good-looking enough to inspire that sort of reaction, and I still obviously felt jumpy around him, even though we'd been dating for weeks. In fact, I seemed to be more nervous now than I had been at first.

The first few times we went out, I had been excited and nervous. Now that the newness was gone, the excitement had faded, too. But the nervousness never left.

At the sound of another motor, I looked out front again, but it wasn't Brian; it was just Jeff in his stupid convertible. Evan and Alicia pulled themselves out of the tiny backseat, and I wondered how they had managed to fit their backpacks and pillows into the space where their legs should have been. Oh well, that was not my problem. Waving good-bye to their dad, they lugged their stuff up to the house.

"Hi, Mom." Alicia gave me a quick hug.

"Can I make popcorn?" Evan asked.

"After you take your stuff up to your room." I wanted to make him give me a hug, too, but these things can't be forced now that he's getting so big.

He looked hopefully at me. "Dad promised I could watch *Creature Feature*."

"At my house?"

"Well, no. But we didn't have time last night. . ."

"It's not anything gory, is it?"

He shook his head. "Only a giant moth destroying downtown Tokyo."

"Okay, put your stuff away and then you can watch it."

He dashed away, banging his backpack full of dirty clothes into the stair railing as he bounded up the stairs.

Alicia threw her jacket at the nearest hook on the wall. "He was really afraid you wouldn't let him watch it."

"I think he's old enough for Mothra, don't you?"

"No, not that. But you told him he couldn't watch TV for a week. Because he kept leaving his clothes on the bathroom floor."

"Oh, yeah." So he snuck that one by me. Should I retract my permission or carry it over until later? Either way, he wasn't getting off. And I didn't like this evidence of dishonesty on his part.

Alicia pulled a bag of tortilla chips out of the cabinet. "He was all set to watch at Dad's until Dad told us to

pack up our stuff because we had to come home early."
She unrolled the bag, pulled out a chip, and examined it
as if she could tell whether it was stale by the shape of the
edges. "Do we have any salsa?"

I nodded toward the refrigerator. "So you didn't know
about this either? Coming home early?"

"No, but I should have guessed."

"Why?"

Alicia leaned closer and lowered her voice. "Dad and
Linda are having Stage Two Commitment Difficulties."

"What the. . .did they tell you that?"

"No, but it's obvious to anyone who sees them together.
They're taking a trip up to Deep Creek Lake to reconnect."

"Isn't that special," I said sarcastically, allowing myself
a minute to fume. I had suggested Deep Creek to Jeff as
a family vacation spot at least once, with no success. He
always said he couldn't take the time off.

"Time without the distractions of home and family
will allow them to work through the problems in their
relationship in a nonhostile environment," she recited
very clinically.

I wanted to ask just what sort of problems they
were having, hoping maybe it was husband-beating or
something equally painful to Jeff's ego. But I couldn't put
my daughter in the middle of that. So instead I asked
about her diagnosis as I reached for a handful of chips.
"You sound very official. Have you matched them up with
a test in one of your magazines?"

She nodded. "Yes. They fit the profile of 'Dating
Difficulties' from the August issue of *Teen Life*."

"Except they're not dating. They're married now."

"Whatever. There are lots of couples who've been dating longer than Dad and Linda have been married."

I choked as I inhaled the corner of a chip. "Couples you know? In middle school?"

"They've only been married a year, Mom."

"Still, I don't think of long-term relationships. . .do you analyze them, too? Other students, I mean."

"Yeah, sometimes." She suddenly seemed very interested in the bag of chips. Then she began carefully wiping the rim of the salsa jar.

"Do lots of girls in your class have boyfriends?" I asked softly.

She shrugged, her gaze still focused on the jar as if the secrets of life lay therein.

"You know, it's not really much use having a boyfriend until you're old enough to drive. Otherwise you have to have your mom drive you on dates."

She smiled at the jar as she picked at a piece of dried onion on the rim.

"So if you're worried because you don't have one, don't be. It'll happen when the time is right." And twelve was not the right time, it was *way* too young, but saying that might make her all the more determined to go find a boyfriend.

She looked up, flipping her hair back out of her face. "So what's wrong between you and Brian?"

"Me and Brian? Nothing." I reached for the salsa. That piece of dried onion on the rim of the jar really needed attention.

"You don't look happy when his name comes up."

I put on a smile. "Of course I do."

"That's convincing."

I let the smile sag. Just how much had she noticed? How unhappy did I look? How long had I looked unhappy?

Was I unhappy?

"Is he unwilling to commit?" she asked matter-of-factly as she dunked a chip into the jar.

"We haven't come that far," I admitted as I picked up the chip bag. "Though I don't think he's the 'fear of commitment' type." I couldn't believe I was discussing this with my twelve-year-old.

She nodded. "Maybe you're the one who has a problem with commitment."

"Maybe *Teen Life* needs to find writers who can branch out a little. Not every problem has to do with commitment, you know."

"That's what people think. But every problem can be traced back to difficulty with commitment."

"Look, Brian has no problem committing to a relationship. He was happily married for years. He just has a problem finding time for me, I think, because he's got so many other things going on. His days are so tightly scheduled—I bet his calendar looks like an encyclopedia. Each day's entry would take up a whole page."

"You mean like our calendar?" Alicia waved toward the bulletin board.

"No, I mean he's got activities for every. . ." the words died in my throat as I looked at the calendar on the wall. Evan's indoor soccer games and Cub Scout meetings, Alicia's drama classes, the bookfair at school, days when I was on assignment at the Blue Moon—it was a pretty full schedule. I complained about how little time I had to do chores or spend time with my kids. My days were as busy as Brian's, and my complaining about his schedule was the pot calling the kettle black. I had no right to resent him giving time to "his" kids just as I did.

But I had been doing just that. And then I'd feel bad about it, just as I did now. And then I'd worry that I couldn't say anything because I was afraid I'd say something I'd regret, so I just wouldn't talk.

Which made me too quiet. Too dull.

Brian would get tired of me if I was too dull.

"Why are you doing that?" Alicia asked.

"Doing what?" I looked down at my hands.

"Breaking that chip into little tiny pieces. That's a sign of relationship frustration, you know."

"Which issue is that from?"

"July, I think."

I set the crumbs down on the counter. "If you must know, I'm afraid I'm boring him. I get all upset, but then I don't want to be upset, so I just. . ."

"Start playing with your food?"

"Yeah, I guess." This time wasn't the only time a date had ended badly. The last time Brian came over for dinner, I stopped talking just like I had tonight. I was afraid to say the wrong thing. But saying nothing was bad, too.

Alicia smiled. "Just be yourself, Mom. If you're nervous."

"I'm acting nervous?"

"Yeah."

"Is that from the July issue, too?"

She shook her head. "They say that in practically every issue. 'He'll like you for yourself if he's worth liking at all.'"

Would he like a whining, complaining, tyrannical woman? I didn't like myself half the time. How could I expect him to like me for who I was?

"Are you crying, Mom?" Alicia enfolded me in a hug. I sniffed. "No."

"Crying is good for you. It cleans your tear ducts."

I didn't know if crying was so great, but hugging my daughter sure was. When had she become so wise? Her comfort and reassurance flowed into me with a surprising warmth, strengthening me. I wanted to thank someone for giving me such a wonderful girl, for the gift of a daughter's love that was proving to be as powerful and healing as a mother's love.

Who should I thank? Her? God?

Heavy footsteps thundered down as Evan bounded down the stairs. "Mom, where's the popcorn?"

"Same place it always is." I reluctantly released my hold on Alicia.

He looked at me with concern. "Did someone die?"

"No," I sniffed. I still felt a knot in my stomach, despite Alicia's calming influence. Maybe that's why Brian stopped having dinner with me. Maybe every time we had time to talk, I turned into a nervous wreck. It couldn't be any more fun for him than it was for me. Maybe it was my problems holding us back, not his.

I hoped this was one of those instances where they say recognizing the problem is half the solution. I could have asked Alicia, since this was doubtless another topic covered in one of her magazines. But I couldn't rely on my daughter for everything. I guess I'd always relied on Jeff, back when we were together. I didn't feel close enough to my parents to talk to them about much more than the weather and Evan's soccer scores. And I didn't want to start paying for a psychologist.

I opened the pantry and grabbed the dog's leash. "C'mon, Tara." I would share my problems with the family canine.

After spending the weekend trying to explain to my dog why I was so unpleasant to be around and then a Monday of simply *being* unpleasant to be around (because Rodney had moved everything in the office and my attempt to speak with Carl at the firehouse failed because he was out on a call), I welcomed the chance to come into the Blue Moon on Tuesday with one goal firmly in mind. I would convince Eric to confess that he was responsible for the damage.

I arrived before the store opened; indeed, most of the storefronts on Main Street were dark except for the coffee shops. It was actually not much after nine; the stores wouldn't open for a while. Bracing myself against the December wind, I walked up to the end of the block, around the corner, and down the alley behind the stores. There was no sign of life outside any of them, including the auction gallery and the Blue Moon. I tried the steel door and was rewarded with the sound of accusatory dog barks. Mr. P. was keeping his dog there at night. I wondered whether he was still spending nights on the couch in the office while I, who had been hired to stop the vandalism, slept soundly in my bed.

Soon, Mr. P. And dog, I promised. *I'll make the case soon.*

This would have been a very good time for Eric to show up; I could question him in private so he wouldn't be embarrassed. Dave had a terrific ability to convince people to confess, and I know a large part of his strategy involved making the target feel at ease. The back alley and storeroom, where Eric was used to working, would certainly be an atmosphere to put him at ease.

But Eric decided not to make things easy on himself, arriving at the front of the store about the same time as Vicki. Mr. P. had noticed me at the front door and let me in about twenty minutes earlier. I saw no more damaged paintings or antiques. If anything, things looked to be in better shape than when I'd last been there.

Eric hurried ahead to open the door for Vicki, and she rewarded him with one of her "thank you for flying with us" smiles.

"Mr. P., you look exhausted," she gushed as she stashed her green leather handbag under the counter.

He chuckled. "Thanks. You look great, too."

"You're still sleeping in the office, aren't you?" She wagged a finger at him. "Mrs. P. is going to get the wrong idea!"

"Ah," he waved away her objection, "she gets a lotta wrong ideas." He lowered his voice and leaned closer to both of us. "It's working. We've had no new damage since Buster and I started staying here nights."

"I think the dog alone would do it," Vicki noted. "He sounds so fierce."

Mr. P. yawned. "Maybe." He shuffled back toward the office.

"Oh, no." Vicki frowned at the other side of the room. "That doesn't look right at all."

Before I could ask her what didn't look right, she came out from behind the counter and strode over to the opposite wall to gaze up critically at the paintings. While I hurried over to make sure she hadn't discovered another damaged painting, Vicki went to the back of the store and carried out a ladder. After testing the hinges to make sure the ladder was locked in the open position, she climbed gracefully to the top, plucked the dead tree picture from its hanger, and carried it carefully down.

"The light is all wrong there," she explained.

"Yeah, I can see there wasn't enough light to keep the tree alive." My feeble attempt at a joke.

She seemed not to notice, or maybe she was just being kind. "I think maybe over here. . ." She walked several paces toward the front of the store and held up the painting. "Yes, that's good. More natural light, but not too much."

I decided not to bother asking whether that was enough light to bring the tree back to life.

"I still think it looks like one of those Tollefsens."

"It's much better than a Tollefsen."

The artist's own mother couldn't have been more proud. While she was fussing with the painting, I decided to see if I could find Eric. He wasn't in the workroom in the back, and I didn't see him out in the alley. But when I went to the front door to see just how far I'd have to run if I made a quick dash down the street to get a cup of coffee, I found Eric working in the corner of the window display.

"Didn't see you there," I remarked, which was stupid, because it was finally seeing him that made me say something.

"Yeah." He looked a little embarrassed. "I noticed this morning that there were a lot of fingerprints on this glass table. It looked pretty sloppy from outside."

"The table looks great from here."

"Well, yeah, when I finished with that, I thought I might as well polish up these lampshades a bit, too." As he spoke, he rubbed some leaded glass shades firmly with a rag.

"That looks like hard work."

"Not too bad," he said, grunting with exertion. He worked as if he felt guilty for hurting his employer.

I glanced to the back. Vicki was offering the dog a piece of her breakfast bagel and Mr. P. was nowhere in sight. "Hey, can I talk to you for a minute?"

"I guess."

"Mr. and Mrs. P. are pretty upset about the merchandise that's been getting damaged lately." I decided to play up the guilt.

"Yeah, I guess they are."

"I sure would be, wouldn't you? Watching your investments getting ruined? Not being able to report it to insurance because you have no idea how it's happening? They've lost a ton of money."

He looked at me fully for the first time, his eyes wide with disbelief. "They haven't reported it to their insurance company?"

I shook my head. "No. They're afraid the company will cancel."

His attention turned back to the glass as he murmured softly, "I thought it would be. . ."

"What?" I tried to keep my voice gentle, not accusatory.

He cleared his throat. "I thought the insurance company would cover the loss."

"In which case the damage wouldn't hurt Mr. and Mrs. P., but just some big corporation?"

"Yeah."

"Well, that's not the case."

He was cracking, I could see that.

"Maybe, if they knew how or why the damage occurred and could assure the insurance company that it wouldn't happen again. . ."

"Well. . ." He cleared his throat and shifted his weight from one foot to the other. "I can do that."

"You can?"

"Yes. I damaged the dining room set. And the lamp."

"You. . ." even though I had been certain he was guilty, I was stunned that he confessed so readily. "Why?"

He glanced toward the back of the store. "I can't tell you. I don't need to tell you, do I?"

Well yes, he probably did. "Not for the moment," I allowed.

He folded the rag in his hands, almost as if he were uttering a prayer. "It was a really bad idea. I never should have agreed—I never should have done it. I promise it won't happen again."

"You said you damaged the dining room set. And a lamp. Was there anything else?"

He squeezed his eyes shut. "There was a clock, too. I broke off a piece of the molding."

"Is that all?"

"Isn't that enough?" His eyes brimmed over with tears. "It won't happen again. I promise."

"You'll need to talk to Mr. and Mrs. P. But we'll wait a bit, until you're ready," I added quickly. I debated telling the store owners about Eric's confession myself, but decided to hold off for a while. What if Dave's suspicion was correct? What if Mr. and Mrs. P. were involved somehow, damaging their own merchandise for reasons I had yet to figure out?

This wasn't all of the story, not by a long shot. Eric had mentioned nothing about the damaged paintings, although he must have known about them. All he seemed to think of was his own guilt and remorse. But he wasn't working alone, that was plain. Before anything came out in the open, I needed to find out who he was working with. And why.

10

"M om?" Evan asked in his "I'm-being-nice-because-I-
want-something" voice. "Can we put up the Christmas tree today?"

I sighed. Evan's voice had interrupted my imaginary
confrontation with Sarah, who, I concluded, had per-
suaded Eric to damage antiques so they could be sold
for less. In my scenario, Eric fixed the broken goods and
Sarah arranged sales to someone else, maybe even another
dealer.

My imaginary confrontation turned ugly, however,
when the imaginary Sarah pointed out that imaginary Eric
was fixing the broken antiques at the Blue Moon, *before*
they were sold to anyone else. So it was just as well that
Evan interrupted the scene before I made an imaginary
fool out of myself.

But he had reminded me of another big item on my
never-ending "to do" list. When was I going to find time
to get all the Christmas stuff out of the basement? I smiled
sadly. "Not today."

"Then can I watch TV?"

Evan was hopping on one foot, balancing an empty
corn chip bag on the other foot.

I glanced suspiciously at the evidence of unauthorized
junk food consumption. "Did I say you could have
those?"

"They were leftover from my lunch. So can I?"

"Can you what?" I was still angry at the imaginary

Sarah for ruining my theory about her guilt.

"Can I watch TV?"

"Have you done your homework?"

He nodded.

"Cleaned your room?"

"Yes."

"You're sure? That includes putting your clothes away. And shutting the drawers."

"Yep." He hopped over to the trash can and kicked the empty wrapper into it. "Two points!"

"What are you going to watch?"

He shrugged. "I dunno."

I should have been making dinner, but I hadn't been able to think about anything other than Eric's confession, so even the effort to decide what to make for dinner was too much. I gave up staring unseeingly into the kitchen cabinets and followed Evan downstairs to the basement family room so I could keep an eye on his TV selections.

As he flipped to a channel with a man standing in a boat holding up a largemouth bass, he turned to me. "Looks kinda like Alicia, doesn't it?"

A small laugh escaped my lips and I nodded. I shouldn't have agreed, but there was something about the expression on the fish's face that reminded me of the look on Alicia's face when I check to make sure she's up in the morning.

Evan next flipped to a cartoon involving a family of talking dolphins. My mind drifted back to Eric again. If he hadn't damaged the paintings, who had? And why?

For that matter, why had he damaged the antiques? And such insignificant damage, really, compared to the paintings. Broken molding that could be glued back on with little difficulty. Broken glass that could be replaced. The paintings, on the other hand, needed very costly repairs if they weren't totally ruined.

Evan flipped to a channel where contestants were apparently having their jewelry creations evaluated by a panel of judges who seemed to take great delight in insulting everything brought before them.

"Did you hear that, Mom?" Evan giggled. "He said it looked like she vomited on a piece of glass and made it into a necklace."

I grimaced. The next judge said he wouldn't even give the necklace to his dead grandmother. The third judge pointed out that the piece might still have a great deal of intrinsic value, because the contestant had incorporated rare glass and large pieces of jade into it.

"Jade in an ugly setting is still jade," the judge commented in what I was certain was a fake British accent.

Once they heard it was valuable, the other judges gave the necklace more respect. At least their insults weren't quite so vulgar.

Why had that caught my attention? The case at the Blue Moon involved no jewelry at all.

But it did involve things of value. The damaged paintings, at least some of them, were worth far more than the furniture. No furniture had been damaged recently—only paintings. Were the paintings the real target? Did someone damage the furniture just to confuse investigators?

Had I been watching too many suspense shows on TV? No one did stuff just to confuse investigators. Did they?

I sat back and looked around for popcorn. Regardless of why the furniture had been damaged, since the paintings were worth more and so much more difficult, if not impossible, to repair, they should have been my focus all along. They would be my focus now.

So was Eric lying? Or was he clueless about the real problem?

I needed popcorn and a Diet Coke to help me think.

As the TV volume got louder and a commercial for Hamburger Helper flashed across the screen, I realized it was dinnertime and microwave popcorn was not suitable dinner food, however much I want to convince myself to the contrary.

We didn't have any hamburger, but we did have cans of tuna stored with the other warehouse-club boxes in the laundry room. The cans were dustier than I'd expected, so I stepped into the bathroom to rinse them off before carrying them upstairs.

"Evan, you left the toilet seat up again."

"I did not!" he yelled back indignantly.

"No one else could have done it," I pointed out. Neither his sister nor I had any reason to raise the seat except to clean, and that certainly hadn't happened recently.

"Well I didn't do it." His voice was firm, his expression sullen, but his gaze was still focused on the TV. I marched over to hit the power button with a can of tuna.

"Hey!"

"If you're going to lie to me, you're going to lose TV time. Starting now."

"It's not fair," he wailed, now finally looking at me. "You blame me for everything."

I bit back my retort. I was the evil, punishing mother, so naturally he was going to complain. I had to let it go or we would never have dinner.

Once the casserole was in the oven, I glanced at the calendar. Scouts tonight, that uniform was clean. But there was an indoor soccer game tomorrow night—was that one clean? I went upstairs to Evan's room to check.

When I flipped on the light, I was greeted with a scene of utter fashion mayhem. Clothes lay strewn across the bed and hung out of open dresser drawers as if caught in the act of trying to escape. "Evan!" I bellowed toward the stairs.

He was in the basement and of course could not hear me, which made me even madder. I marched down one flight of stairs. "Evan!"

Still no answer.

Down the basement steps. "EVAN!"

He was lying on the couch playing with a portable video game and literally jumped several inches at the sound of my angrier-than-usual voice.

"You said you cleaned your room!"

"I did!" he insisted.

"No, you didn't. There are clothes everywhere."

"I picked up all the clothes."

Marching over to the couch, I reached for his arm. "Come with me."

He scurried out of my reach, but did at least head for the stairs. Bounding up, two at a time, he reached the bedroom ahead of me, but not by much. Anger is unfortunately one of my most powerful motivators.

"I picked up all the clothes off the floor, see?" he announced.

"But you just put them on the bed."

"I'm going to wear them tomorrow."

"Not all of them."

"Yes." He nodded emphatically. "It's really cold in my school."

"What about those over there?" I waved toward the dresser.

"I forgot."

"Well put them away."

He grabbed a loose sleeve and pushed a sweatshirt back into its drawer.

"Not like that! You'll get everything all wrinkled." With a sigh of exasperation, I stepped over to the dresser, snatched the shirt from his hands, and demonstrated how to fold it. "You have to refold all of them. You've made a complete mess."

The Game Boy beeped from somewhere in the pocket of his hooded sweatshirt.

"Give me that," I demanded, holding out my hand.

"Why?"

"Because you've lost the privilege of using it."

"It's not fair!" He smacked the video toy into my hand.

"You lied to me. You told me you picked up your room."

"I did!"

"If that's what you think, then you're lying to yourself as well as to me." Though I was trying hard to keep my voice in check, my anger was rising more with every denial. I turned and left before I gave in to the urge to pack up all his clothes and donate them to Goodwill.

We had this battle almost every day and I was getting tired of it.

But it was worse than just a messy room and wrinkled clothes. Evan was lying to me, telling me things that weren't true. I couldn't trust him anymore. And that hurt more than I wanted to admit.

⁓

When the phone rang after dinner, the caller ID told me it was Brian. I glanced guiltily at the copy of *Teen Life* magazine I had been looking through. Did I have a problem with commitment, as Alicia suggested? It almost seemed like Brian was calling to discuss the issue. I stared at the phone stupidly for two more rings before I answered.

"Hello?"

"Hi, Karen, it's Brian." He paused. "I was expecting to get the answering machine."

"No, uh, you've got me." *The question is, do you want me?*

"So, how've you been?"

"Good." Almost without realizing it, I began to wrap the phone cord around the top of a kitchen chair.

"Glad to hear it. How's work been?"

"Good." *Well, not really, since I'd almost been fired,* but I decided he probably really didn't want to hear the gory details.

"That's. . .great. Everything okay with the kids?"

"Yeah, fine." *Except that my son is turning into a pathological liar and my daughter is trying to analyze everyone with information that is probably way beyond her years.*

"How's soccer going?"

"For Evan?" The phone cord was now twisted so tightly around the chair back that I was having a hard time untangling it. "He hasn't had any games yet this week. He has one tomorrow."

"Wish I could come. But I've got basketball practice."

"I figured as much."

For a moment, neither of us said anything more.

I'm boring him.

I cleared my throat. Most people liked to talk about themselves, didn't they? I could try that. "So how has your workweek been?"

"Busy," he said, sounding relieved to have something to say. "We acquired a company in California and the team there is used to doing things differently. We have to recode everything they submit."

"Oh, that sounds. . .frustrating." I didn't know enough about his work to have a clue what he was talking about, and that was indeed frustrating, for me at least.

"It is. And the specs they're sending out don't make any sense at all, so we can't even change those without going over everything with one of their engineers. It takes forever."

"Oh, no." I tried to sound interested and sympathetic. Not sure I succeeded, but maybe I did because he continued talking.

"My boss wants to send a group of us out there to meet with them in person, but that's only going to take more time, with travel and all."

I murmured something sympathetic again as I finished untangling the phone cord from the chair. I turned away from the chair and focused my gaze out the living room window, sitting on my hands so they couldn't stray toward the phone cord again. I was coming dangerously close to disconnecting the phone, and then Brian would think I wasn't listening. Really wasn't listening, not just sort-of-wasn't-listening like now.

"Are you coming to practice on Friday? I promise to have Diet Coke for you this time."

He suddenly had my attention, and it wasn't just the promise of carbonation and caffeine. Was I going to the rehearsal? I hadn't decided. Evan was sleeping over at a friend's. Alicia had plans. So I had no good reason not to go.

In the silence I could hear Brian breathe softly into the phone receiver.

"Um, yeah," I said at last, not even aware of my decision until the words came out of my mouth. "I think I can make it, as long as I don't stay too late."

"Great." Relief sounded in his voice.

I decided to take it a step further. "How about if we meet a little early, just the two of us?" I suggested. "The kids are getting picked up at six and I could come to the church right after that." This would make the rehearsal a little more like what I'd envisioned from the beginning. We'd have time to talk some. But it wouldn't be a whole night of time alone, like the disastrous dinner dates. Maybe I'd stop being so nervous around him.

"Great idea. I'll be there at six."

"Well, I can't get there *right* at six unless I teleport from my house."

"That's okay. I'll wait for you."

I liked the warmth in his voice as he said that. The

neighbor's porch light came on, spilling light through the window that sparkled through the remains of the crystal cross Brian had given me. Even broken, the ornament could still be beautiful and could still reflect light. Maybe this was a sign that we would be able to work things out. I smiled. "See you Friday, then."

"You bet. Keep the faith!"

We hung up. A shadowy figure passed by outside the window, accompanied by a deep rumbling noise. The neighbor taking out his trash. Soon the light went out and the cross was just a broken piece of glass once more. I decided to take it down.

And I was pretty sure now that I knew who had broken it, even if he insisted he was innocent.

11

I almost ran into Brittany's desk when I went into the office on Thursday. I was the first one there. It was dark and, for some reason, her new desk had been moved so that it was at an angle almost directly in front of the door. When I flipped on the light, I felt like I was entering the rain forest exhibit at the public aquarium. The three support columns that helped hold up the ceiling of the old place had been covered with plants. Completely covered. Hanging plants on all sides, potted palms on the floor, even some of those little "air plants" that are supposed to survive without soil were sitting on little plastic shelves attached to the columns. Rodney's fountain was gurgling up a storm—weren't these things supposed to be turned off when no one was there?

I decided that instead of being energy-efficient and unplugging the source of the Amazon or whatever it was supposed to be, I would head to the opposite corner of the office, to the old closet we had converted to a tiny kitchen.

The coffeemaker was gone, and a computer sat in its place of honor on the counter. Even the counter was different—the stained white Formica had been replaced with textured terra-cotta tile. The pine cabinet fronts and brass drawer pulls had been polished clean of years of popcorn grease, newspaper ink, and other grime. While I admired the look, the kitchen was apparently unable to fulfill its basic purpose: to provide a never-ending source of caffeine.

I was still searching through the cabinets for the missing coffeemaker when I heard the office door open.

"Dave?" I called hopefully.

"It's me," Brittany called. "Brittany," she added for clarification.

"Do you know where the coffeepot is?" I asked as I turned around and headed back into the office.

She shook her head. "I don't drink coffee."

"Do you know why there's a computer on the kitchen counter?" Without giving her a chance to answer, I waved around the room. "What's going on here?"

"Ooh, I can't remember what it's called." She bit her lip in concentration. "Funk spray? Something like that."

"Huh?"

Her face reddened. "I said I can't really remember. Ask Rodney, he did it all."

"Yeah, I will ask him. But shouldn't we move your desk away from the door first? I almost impaled myself on a letter opener."

She shook her head. "Rodney said everything is mathematically arranged to take advantage of the principles of. . .funk spray or whatever. He gets real upset when Dave moves things."

"You haven't *seen* upset yet," I muttered.

"Yeah." She gave me a nervous look and then glanced toward Dave's office. "We'd better find that coffeepot."

I finally sent Brittany out to the Kirinyaga tearoom for coffee, wishing I could afford to get us both lattes, but settling for two regular coffees. While she was gone, I rechecked every cabinet, drawer, and cubbyhole, glancing up at every sound to see whether it might be Dave or Rodney arriving.

Rodney came first. I heard the crisp tap of his hard-soled shoes walking across the gouged pine floors.

"You're late!" I challenged as I rolled out to greet him.

"I had a meeting." He hung his coat on the strange rack of blue padded knobs that replaced the antler coatrack.

"A meeting?"

"With our new client, Consolidated Building."

"Oh." It was looking even more likely that Rodney had brought in that account on his own, which would make him very valuable. Dave might be willing to forgive the sudden influx of plants and fountains.

But not the removal of the coffeemaker.

"Why isn't the coffeepot on the kitchen counter?"

"That counter is the point farthest to the southeast."

"Yes, and the weather today is partly cloudy, but that hasn't caused me to move any major appliances."

"A coffeemaker is a small appliance, Mrs. Maxwell."

"It's a major appliance at this time of the morning. And it happens to be a major appliance that *I* bought. So why is there a computer in its place?"

"Since that computer is used for billing purposes that generate income for the firm, it is most optimally located in the southeastern portion of the office."

"Even if that part of the office happens to be the kitchen?"

He shrugged. "A room may be whatever we choose to make of it."

"When a room has plumbing and a refrigerator, we choose to make it a kitchen." I sighed and rubbed at my temple where I could feel a headache building. "So do you expect Brittany to work in the tiny closet kitchenette that doesn't even have room for a chair?"

"No, of course not. Her computer is right there." He pointed to the rolltop desk I'd dodged earlier. "It's your computer that's in the kitchen."

"What?" The word exploded out of my mouth, and I wanted to really let him have it then, for ruining the office, wasting our money, and most of all invading my privacy. But just as I was about to let loose, I had the strange sensation that that was exactly what he expected me to do, and that it wouldn't do any good. He would brush off my complaints like he was brushing dog hair from a gabardine suit. I would instead gather ammunition and take my complaints to Dave, who had the power to actually do something about them. Like fire the guy.

"So," I said in the sweetest voice I could manage without caffeine, "explain to me how putting my computer in the kitchen will benefit DS Investigations."

"It's quite simple, really. According to the principles of feng shui. . ."

Aha! Funk spray!

". . .a computer that is used to generate income should be placed in the southeast section of the office, while a computer placed in the north or west will enhance creativity."

"Northwest?" I glanced to the opposite side of the building. That would be Dave's office. "But Dave's work generates income. So shouldn't *his* computer be in the kitchen?"

Rodney's smile faltered. "Well, we have to draw distinctions somewhere. The north side of the office is where we place our symbols of business success." He pointed to a fishbowl and what appeared to be a red envelope on a table between Dave's office and his own cubicle.

"I see." I decided to give him a compliment before finding out where he was holding the coffeepot hostage. "I like what you've done with the kitchen. The new counters are pretty."

"The rough, natural surface balances the smooth white walls."

"And will hide crumbs, too. But we really do need our coffeemaker."

"Since it's so important to you, we could move it to your desk."

"Oh. Er, thank you." I guess. It was going to be very crowded in there. "So what do all these plants do?"

"They redirect the energy that would be blocked by those unsightly, squared-off poles."

"Okay. And why did you move Brittany's desk?"

"With her desk against the wall, it blocked the flow of energy."

I nodded. "Whereas now it just blocks the people who want to come into the office."

"The desk is angled, so that energy can flow uninterrupted."

"If we moved it back a few feet, then people could flow uninterrupted, too."

"Ah, but then it would be directly in line with the negative energy from the door, which is bad feng shui."

"Okay, then." This seemed to bolster my earlier argument about keeping the door locked, but I decided not to press the point. "Do you think the fountain needs to run all the—"

"Hey everybody!" Dave threw open the door, neatly sidestepped Brittany's desk, and bounded into the center of the room holding two plastic grocery bags. "I made the Alfonso case. Two weeks ahead of when I'd predicted." He reached into one of the bags and pulled out cans of Pringles. He tossed the first one to me.

"That's terrific!" I surprised myself by catching the chips one-handed. Dave's mood was contagious. I knew he'd been worried about this case, or at least as worried as he ever gets.

"They've promised us a bonus, since we'll be billing fewer hours."

"Even better." I opened the chips. If I wasn't getting coffee, I might as well enjoy something. "Not many clients will go that far."

"Well, I saved them a lot of money. They owe us. Anyone like jalapeno?" He waved a can with red and green stripes.

"I'm good with plain ones." I held up my red can.

"Do you have any sour cream and onion?" Brittany asked.

Dave shook his head. "How about these with jokes printed on them?"

"Cool." She reached for the blue and red can he handed her.

"Mr. Sarkesian?" Rodney asked.

"You want jalapeno?"

He grimaced. "No, thank you, not at this hour of the morning." He cast a longing glance toward Dave's office. "I was simply going to suggest that since you have unforeseen time available, this might be the opportune moment to release the trapped energy in your office."

"Huh?"

I nodded toward Dave. "I think he means you need to clean up the mess."

"The boxes and other detritus block the flow of energy," Rodney explained.

Dave waved him off as he started back toward his office. "How about if I close the door and the energy can just stay out here, where you've got things arranged so it can race around like the cars in the Daytona 500?"

"But your office space needs energy, too."

"Got lots of energy," Dave insisted through a mouthful of chips. He turned and held up one of the Pringles cans. "Look at the carbohydrate count in just one serving."

"Can I talk to you for a moment?" I hurried after him.

"Sure." He waved me forward. When he reached his desk, he slung a plastic bag with a few more cans of chips onto his credenza and then slid into his chair. "What's up?"

I closed the door carefully behind me. Then I turned to face my brother. "He's got to go."

"Who?"

"He unplugged the coffeemaker."

"Rodney?"

"He moved my computer into the kitchen."

"Oh, yeah, I figured you probably hadn't done that."

"He is spending a fortune on fancy lights, fountains, plants, and who knows what else."

Dave rubbed his hand across the stubble on his chin. "Yeah, but he's brought in enough new business to cover the extra expense."

A sick feeling settled in the pit of my stomach. Rodney

had brought Consolidated Building to our firm. Dave would reward him by assigning cases to him instead of me.

"Besides," he continued as he wiped his greasy hands on a napkin, "I like plants. As long as someone else waters them."

"I'm not doing it."

"One of the other two will manage. Now, I'm sorry Rodney moved your computer. If you'd like, I'll get you a new one."

I stared at him in shock. "He must have brought in a lot of money for you to make that offer. I've been hinting for a new computer for two years now, and you always bring up some excuse about cash flow."

"So, good—you'll be happy with a new computer, and Rodney will be happy with a computer in the kitchen."

"And it's important to keep Rodney happy because. . .?"

Dave shrugged. "I like him."

"I don't buy it."

"I like lots of people."

"Yes, but you'd never actually spend money to keep them happy."

Dave looked at me pointedly as he sat back in his chair. "Don't you have some work to be doing? Tell me what's going on at the Blue Moon."

Since he was paying me, I guess it was time to stop asking the questions and start answering them. I sat down on the edge of his desk. "I know who's been damaging the antiques."

"Great. Now you should try to finesse a confession."

"He's already confessed. To me, at least."

Dave smiled as he reached back into the bag to retrieve

a can of chips. "That's great. Now all you have to do is to coax—"

I held up my hand. "He only confessed to damaging antiques. But I think the real issue is the damage to the paintings. They're worth a lot more than the furniture and they can't be easily repaired." I debated telling him that additional paintings had been damaged since I started the case. But it was in my report; he could read it himself. It would be my way to see if he really did read my activity reports.

"But there were more antiques damaged, weren't there? And only three paintings."

"Well, five now," I admitted. "We found damage to two more last week."

"While you've been on assignment?" He let out a low whistle. "That can't have made them too happy."

"An understatement. I even offered to resign."

He winced.

"Yeah, I know that's not how you would have handled it. Anyway, they kept me on, obviously. So of the five damaged paintings, three of them are worth a lot of money, because they're by John Tollefsen."

"Never heard of him."

"I think that proves my point. The only artists *you* know are the ones who do cheap comic books."

"Some of their art is worth a lot, too."

"Well, their art isn't hanging in the Blue Moon. Tollefsen's is. And I think it's the focus of the vandalism."

I hadn't realized that was true until I said it. Not just artwork, but Tollefsen's artwork. That was the key. The other stuff, antiques, other paintings, was just to throw us off. Every other picture that had been damaged was near a damaged Tollefsen.

"So what do we know about Tollefsen?"

"Not enough," I admitted. "And I'm going to do something about that right now." I started for the door.

"Without coffee?"

I reached for a can of potato chips. "Hopefully spicy chips will keep my eyes open just as well."

Until I could get a new computer, I was going to have to work in the kitchen. I changed my screensaver to display a dancing fork and then started an Internet search to see what I could learn about John Tollefsen.

I guess he was so popular in this region of the country because he lived here all his life and used local subjects in his work. From what I could tell, all the subjects of his gray surrealistic paintings could have come from an unlit attic or garage anywhere in the country. His best known painting depicted a pair of scissors cutting the headline out of newspaper. I think the only reason it was famous was because the owner of a rival newspaper bought it and used it in an ad campaign. His most famous works had been done in the 1970s. He was still producing and teaching and two of his students had become renowned in their own right. Judith Gross designed award-winning sets in Los Angeles and Craig Freels photographed local subjects in his hometown of Ellicott City, Maryland.

The jalapeno chips suddenly seemed way too hot. I couldn't remember where I knew the name Craig Freels but it had come up, and I was pretty sure it was in connection with the case.

Was there a Craig in Brian's youth group? Maybe I was

just so anxious to make a connection when I saw Ellicott City that I just thought the name Freels seemed familiar.

Think. Freels was not the name of the artist of any of the damaged works. I might have seen his name on another painting, but I really didn't pay much attention to most of the other pictures.

Freels wasn't the name of any other employee. Was he a consignor? The name of a customer? Was I remembering a name on a charge slip? Where had I seen the name?

When I closed my eyes, I remembered, because I could see it in my mind. I had seen it on a painting. The dead tree painting that Vicki was always moving around. She had told me it was by Craig Freels.

It had never been damaged, unless the canvas was weakened by Vicki breathing on it so often as she carried it around. So it probably had no connection to the damaged Tollefsen paintings, right?

But there might be some connection. And right now it was the only thing I had to go on.

12

The next morning, I watched anxiously for Vicki's BMW to pull up near the Blue Moon. I couldn't wait to ask her about the Freels painting she was always moving around. But if I ran up and started asking questions about something inside the shop while she was still outside locking her car, she might get suspicious.

So instead I waited while she said her cheery greetings to me, Mr. P., and Eric (who had let me in so promptly it was almost as if he'd been waiting by the door). She opened the counter drawer to stow her purse, a pink vinyl thing that looked like a miniature shopping bag and seemed scarcely large enough to hold a set of car keys. She fluffed her hair, checked cell phone messages, and looked around to see if Mrs. P. had any lemon drops left. All the while I pretended to be busy cleaning tape adhesive off an ugly ceramic pitcher shaped like a braying donkey. I knew it would be only a matter of time before she moved the painting, since she had to do it before Mrs. P. arrived. But whereas most days it seemed like I couldn't turn around without seeing the painting in her arms, today she seemed to studiously ignore its siren call.

Minutes ticked by on the surprisingly un-antique digital clock that sat by the cash register. Mrs. P. might arrive at any moment, and the opportunity to move the picture would be lost. Then I'd really need a good excuse to ask about it.

The dead tree picture was hanging very low today, just

over a small chest of drawers with pink ceramic knobs.

"I think this pitcher would look great here, don't you?" I asked Vicki as I took the braying donkey (that would look like it was doing something else if you poured anything out of its mouth) over to the chest of drawers. I planted it firmly right in front of the Freels painting. "The light shows off the, uh, donkey's fur to a nice advantage."

Her eyes widened in horror for a brief moment, but to her credit, she quickly recovered and smiled. "The light *is* good there, but I think the piece should be displayed a little higher up for a better perspective." She hurried over and moved the pitcher to a shelf nearby. "See? We can better admire the elegant angle of the handle this way."

The donkey appeared to be sneering down at me from the shelf. "Oh, yes, I see. Very elegant." I made a face at it before I turned back around to Vicki. "It seems a shame not to put something on that chest of drawers, though. Since the light is so good. I guess we shouldn't block the painting, though. . ."

Vicki nodded slowly. "No, we really shouldn't."

"It's a valuable one, isn't it?"

"Oh, yes. The artist was a student of Tollefsen's, but he quickly surpassed his teacher's talent. So this painting will eventually be worth more than all of Tollefsen's put together. Maybe more than everything in the store."

There was an odd gleam in her eye and a breathless excitement in her voice, and I couldn't decide whether she was thrilled by the painting itself or by the fact that it might be worth so much money. What interested her more, talent or cash? Or perhaps it was some heady combination of the two.

Did she think the painting was more likely to sell if she found just the right location?

I cleared my throat. "The artist, Freels, is local, isn't he? Like Tollefsen."

"Yes," she said as she stared intently at the canvas. "Craig studied under Tollefsen at MICA."

"MICA?"

"Maryland Institute College of Art," she explained.

But it was not the name of the school that really got my attention. It was her use of the artist's first name, as if she knew him personally. I opened my mouth to ask if she did, but some instinct made me shut it again. I don't know what I was thinking exactly, how I figured Vicki might be connected with the problems at the gallery or what the damaged paintings might have to do with Freels. Vicki had ample opportunity to damage the Tollefsen paintings, but no motive whatsoever that I could discern. Unless possibly she had studied art repair techniques and could repair and resell the paintings without disclosing the damage? She was familiar with an art school. And one of its students.

Maybe Craig Freels could tell me something about Tollefsen, what advantage might be gained by damaging his work. But how would I find him? His name was completely absent from the judicial system and Maryland Motor Vehicle Association databases. So very likely Freels was not his legal name. Either that or he'd never gotten a driver's license.

I took my cell phone into the tiny employee restroom. It took forever to warm up, with flashing displays and ringing chimes thanking me for using whatever company I was using and telling me it was looking for service. Then it chirped and told me I had a new voicemail message. Only then was it ready to allow me to dial directory assistance. And after all that, I was told there was no listing for a Freels in Ellicott City. He might be anywhere in the area, of course. I could keep calling directory assistance all day guessing at towns and he probably wasn't even listed under that name. The school might have a directory, but I'd need a student ID code of some sort to get into it. And he might not even be a student anymore.

I wondered if Brittany knew any MICA students.

Then I heard Vicki's voice outside and decided not to call Brittany at the moment.

Instead, I went out and checked the phone book at the counter.

"Looking for something?" Vicki asked in a "may I help you" tone of voice. I think she was trying to be helpful, but of course she was anything but.

"Uh, yeah. . ." I scrambled to think of a reason why I needed to leave the store for a long lunch break. "I need to get my nails redone. They're just a mess. I thought there might be a place I could go on my lunch hour. Oh, silly me, this is the residential listings. No wonder I couldn't find anything." Slamming the book closed, I put my hands behind my back so she wouldn't notice that my nails had never been "done" in my life.

"Well, I would recommend DeFoor's Eden, just up the street and around the corner. You can even walk there from here."

"Great." I bit off a smile. This was not even the least bit great, because I needed an excuse to get into my car and drive somewhere. "That day spa might be too pricey for me, though. I think I might check one of the strip malls on Route 40."

She shrugged.

I pulled out the yellow pages and thumbed through the manicure section for a while, hoping she would leave so I could check the residential listings.

Instead, she pulled out a tray of vintage earrings, sat down next to me, and began straightening them.

With a suppressed sigh, I put away the phone book. Next to it was a worn binder labeled "consignments." I pulled the binder out. "Is this where we list stuff when people leave it in the store on consignment?"

"Yes." Vicki nodded. "I should have shown that to you before. If an item sells that has a consignment tag, we look up the number in the book, find the name and address of the consignor, and see what percentage to send them. Then we ask Mrs. P. to make out a check."

I pretended to be only mildly curious when instead I was dying to tear through the pages to see if there was a listing for Craig Freels. His painting might be on consignment.

It occurred to me that if I was the sort of person who prayed a lot, I might pray that there was a listing for Craig in the book. But that was a silly thing to pray for, and God surely had more important matters to attend to. He didn't have time to listen to frivolous prayer requests from divorced women who made up excuses for not going to church.

Vicki might very well sit there untangling earrings for the rest of the day. I considered trying to sneak the phone book into the restroom, but I'd have to ask her to move to even get to it. And then there might not be a listing.

"Okay, God, give me a break," I thought. "Help me stop this mess. Help me prevent anything else from getting damaged. I mean, I'm asking mostly for myself, but this would be good for the clients, too. If there's a connection with Freels, help me find him."

Three pages later, I saw it. "*Lifeline*, oil on canvas, Craig Freels, 8016 Main Street, Apt. 3, Ellicott City, MD 21043." The price was smeared and difficult to read. It might have said $4000 or it might have said $40,000. But that didn't matter. I could read the address quite clearly. It was just down the street, so I could probably walk there in the time it would take to drive and find a parking space.

"I think I might try getting my nails done at your day spa after all," I announced after I oh-so-casually put the consignment book away. "It's a nice day for a walk." Sleet chose that moment to start crackling against the roof, just to make me look like a liar. "Or at least it *was* a nice day," I murmured. "Do you mind if I take lunch early? It might be less crowded now."

"I don't mind. Say hi to Jocelyn for me."

"Of course." I reached for my purse and tried not to frown at the realization that now I would have to spend money to get a manicure before I came back to the store.

Freels's apartment was in a brick building that I think had been an old railroad hotel at one time. The warped front door didn't quite shut all the way, so I was able to get in easily, and since he was in apartment three, and there were only two doors on the first floor, I climbed up the stairs to the second floor. From the worn brown carpeting on the floor and the flickering lighting in the upstairs hallway, I guessed that this place wasn't quite as upscale as some of the ones farther up the hill.

A plastic grocery bag full of trash sat outside the door to number three, and I could hear music that sounded like the background music in Evan's old Dinosaur Stomp video game, but as if played by a garage punk band. If this was what Freels listened to for inspiration, it might explain why his artwork seemed so dark and dead.

I knocked on the door.

"Somebody there?" A young man's voice called out hoarsely. "If ya forgot yer key, it's open, man."

I knocked again.

"Look, I can't get to the door now, I've almost anni-hilated the Guardian of the Blurbaton. Wait. . .almost, almost. . ." A deafening crescendo of guitar music followed. "Got 'im. All right, hold on, I'll be right there."

The door squeaked open to reveal a guy who looked to be in his late teens, with a chubby face and unruly dark hair, wearing an oversize hooded sweatshirt with grease stains on the front. Was this the brilliant artist whose work rivaled Tollefsen's?

"I'm looking for Craig Freels." I tried to smile as pleasantly as possible, despite my concerns about the acrid animal odor coming from the apartment.

"Not here, I'm afraid. In fact," he said as he grinned, "I thought you were him. When you knocked."

"Does he often knock at his own door?"

"Loses his keys all the time. Then I have to stop whatever

I'm doing and let him in."

"Oh, well, that's nice of you."

He shrugged. "That's why I'm here. To help him out, keep the place up, you know." He waved toward a coffee table covered with wadded-up napkins and empty pizza boxes.

"Oh yeah, I see." I fished around in my purse for a note-pad. "Can you tell me where I might be able to find him?"

"No, 'fraid not. He's probably out shooting something. With his camera," he added when he saw me flash a Vicki-esque look of horror at the word *shoot*. "He, um, takes a lot of pictures."

"I thought he was a painter."

"Used to be. Now it's mostly photos. And then he cuts them up and draws on them and stuff. I don't really. . . understand it all."

"Have you lived with him long?"

He laughed. "All my life, off and on. He's my brother." He peered over as if to try to see what I was writing. "D'ya want to come in? Are you a reporter?"

"No." I debated telling him that I was a gallery owner who wanted to host a show or a buyer representing a wealthy client who was interested in his art. Then he would be in a good mood and inclined to tell me whatever I wanted to know. But I hated to get his hopes up for his brother when I knew what I was doing was not going to lead to any sales of his artwork.

"I'm, uh, doing some research about John Tollefsen, actually," I said at last. "Somebody told me that Craig is one of his students." I reached out to shake his hand. "I'm Karen Maxwell."

"I'm Robby." He reached out to give my hand a quick

shake. "Freels, but you probably figured that out."

I smiled. "Yeah." I tried to think of how to get useful information out of the brother without sounding like an investigator. "So, do you paint or shoot with him sometimes?"

He laughed. "Never. I don't get half the stuff he does, or why anyone would pay for it. But they do."

"Must be nice for him, getting paid while he's still in school."

"Oh, he's out now." Robby scratched his ear. "At least I think he is. I haven't seen him going to any classes lately."

"So your brother's not taking classes with Tollefsen anymore?"

"I don't think he's taking any classes. Except I think he goes to yoga on Wednesdays, but that's just because the instructor is really hot."

"So he doesn't have a girlfriend right now?"

"Nah, he's not the girlfriend type. Don't get me wrong, it's not like he doesn't like girls or anything, but he just doesn't want to spend that much time with them." Robby lifted the lid to a pizza box and then dropped it with a disappointed sigh when he saw that it was empty. "Once he dated this rich girl who started following him around everywhere. Always giving him presents like she could buy him or something. Drove him crazy."

Could that have been Vicki? "So she kinda scared him off, huh?"

"Yeah. She still keeps calling, even though it's been more than a year since he told her he doesn't want to see her anymore. And she still leaves presents outside our door."

"That might not be so bad, getting presents."

He shook his head. "It's creepy, man. The girl's obsessed."

"What's her name? Just in case my son ever. . ." I let the words trail off, implying that my son was old enough that I should be on the lookout for this girl.

His nose and forehead scrunched up in thought. "Can't remember. She was pretty, dressed real nice, brought food over all the time."

"What did she look like?"

"She was. . .well, she had. . .I think she had blond hair. Maybe dark blond. And she was. . ." He looked like he was really struggling.

"Tall? Short?" I prompted.

"Yeah. Well, sort of in the middle." He shrugged. "She looked like she coulda been on TV, like one of those people who sell stuff on the shopping channel, jewelry and stuff."

"Okay." I smiled. "If my son ever brings home a girl who looks like she's been on the shopping channel. . ." *I'll freak out because he's only nine.*

"Sorry, I can't remember more. She had a weird sense of humor, though, I remember that."

"Weird?"

"Yeah, like she'd think something was funny or cute or whatever and she'd kinda go crazy over it. Like one time she and Craig saw this frog on the sidewalk down there when they were coming in one night. She thought it was cute or good luck or something because the next thing I know she's buying frogs for him all the time."

Bingo. "Real frogs?"

"No, like frog statues, frog candy and stuff. She even

bought a frog phone, but Craig gave it back to her. Instead of ringing it croaked." He snickered. "Sort of like their relationship."

"Uh, yeah. So Vi—this girl." I coughed, hoping he hadn't noticed that I almost slipped up and said her name. "She doesn't sound like she's willing to give up on your brother. You said she's still leaving gifts?"

"Yeah, I'm pretty sure it's her. Haven't seen her in a while, but we found a big Hershey's kiss outside the door last week, and I don't think it was from the landlord."

"Has she ever gotten upset? Threatened to do something. . .crazy if he won't see her again?" This was a long shot, but it was all I could think of. Vicki might just think she could get revenge on Craig by damaging the work of his favorite teacher.

"Well, she cried a lot when they broke up. Craig said she got hysterical once and begged him to take her back. But I don't think she's gotten real angry or threatened to do anything mean. In fact, she's offered to set up art shows for him twice with some guy her dad knows. I think she's trying to buy him back."

"Has he accepted her offer?"

He shook his head. "Nah, but he's been tempted. Gotta pay the rent and all."

"So, do you expect him back soon?"

"No idea. He could be out for hours, or he might not like the light and come home after only a few minutes. I never know."

"Does he have favorite places to shoot when the, uh, light is like this?"

"The river, probably. He likes the trees down there."

"Any place in particular along the river?"

"Sorry, can't help ya there."

"Does he carry a cell phone?" I asked hopefully.

"Yep. But he never turns it on. Says it's too distracting."

I handed him a card with my name, cell phone number, and a P.O. Box address on it. "If he has time, tell him to give me a call. I'd really appreciate it."

"Sure." He took the card, but I figured it would end up under a pizza box before too long.

I offered a farewell smile. "Hey, thanks for giving me so much information."

Now to find his brother, all I had to do was head for the Patapsco River. The river ran along the edge of the quaint section of town. I could walk there in a matter of minutes and then search along the banks until I found Craig Freels.

The river was only fifty-two miles long. How much time could that take?

13

Rats," I groaned in frustration. "I can't even unzip my jacket!"

"Do you need me to help you, Mommy?" Alicia asked in a little girl voice, clearly enjoying the difficult time I was having with my fake nails. When I went in for the manicure—my justification for taking that early lunch break—the manicurist told me my nails were too broken and brittle to do much with and that adding nail tips would strengthen them. Well, they might be strong now, but they were absolutely useless. Tasks that I'd never given a second thought to before, such as zipping my jacket or dialing a phone, were next to impossible with a big chunk of acrylic at the end of each finger.

"I still think you should have put lightning bolts on them or racing stripes," Alicia mused as she stepped over to me. I watched with envy as she pinched the handle of the zipper between her thumb and forefinger and effortlessly pulled it down.

"Lightning bolts?"

"For work. Because you type so fast."

"Not anymore I won't." Yikes! I hadn't even thought about how I would manage to function in the office. Type with my elbows? Push the copier buttons with my nose?

Wouldn't Rodney love that? He had suggested typing classes for Brittany, not because her hunt-and-peck typing was inefficient, but because it looked unprofessional. I couldn't wait to hear what he'd say about me typing with my knuckles.

I let out a big sigh as I thought about it. Not only had I accomplished nothing today, I would accomplish nothing until the stupid nails came off. I couldn't even dial the phone. And while I could remove them right now, I wouldn't. I had paid $25 for the ridiculous appendages and I couldn't throw them away that quickly. I would have to get $25 worth of suffering from them first.

"They're really pretty, Mom," Alicia said with admiration.

I hadn't realized I was staring at my nails until she spoke.

"You should get them done every week," she continued.

"It costs too much," I said automatically. I started to add that they were a pain in the neck and a waste of money, but then I realized that she was right. They *were* pretty. Pretty counted for something, every once in a while. If Brian wouldn't give me a useless bunch of pretty flowers to look at, I could have a useless bunch of pretty fingernails.

Her eyes clouded with concern as I wearily threw myself into a chair. "What's wrong?" she asked.

"Nothing."

Everything. I raked my hand through my hair, trying to fend off a headache. I hadn't found Craig Freels. I couldn't even say why it was important for me to find Craig Freels. The idea that somehow Vicki was connected to the damaged paintings because of Freels made no sense, so why was I obsessing over it? I had no other leads, that was why. Or rather I did, but I didn't want to pursue them. I knew Eric was guilty, but I wanted to believe he wasn't the real bad guy. I had come up with no reason to think Sarah or Carl might be involved, and neither of them had any real opportunity to get to the paintings. And I didn't want to think that Mr. and Mrs. P. had cut up their own paintings, because that just seemed sick.

But I didn't want Vicki to be the bad guy either.

I needed a big, bad, greedy villain as a suspect—not nice coworkers.

Maybe investigation wasn't such a great job after all.

I had ruined my shoes tromping up and down the riverbank, even though I only tried for a few minutes before I decided my "lunch break" was getting suspiciously long.

At the office, Dave was replacing me with a funk spray fanatic.

And *now* I needed my daughter's help to undress. Could Alzheimer's be far behind?

As if to underscore my point about brain damage, a searing pain shot through my forehead from one side to the other, as if I'd been electrocuted. When my vision cleared, I realized that one side of my face was tingling. And Evan was standing in front of me with a soccer ball and a guilty expression.

"Sorry, Mom."

I touched my hand to the side of my face, where I was guessing I'd been hit with the ball. "What were you doing?"

"I didn't mean to. It was an accident."

"What were you accidentally doing?"

"I didn't mean to."

"You were kicking the ball in the house, weren't you?" It was either that, or he'd put a motor inside the ball. I didn't think he was that mechanically inclined.

"I wasn't *kicking* it."

"So the ball slipped out of your hands and hit me in the face?"

"You said I couldn't *kick* it."

"Yes, and you disobeyed me."

"I didn't kick it."

"Well, I know I didn't. And Alicia was right next to me so I know she didn't."

"I had the ball, but I wasn't kicking it. I was just moving it."

I rolled my eyes. "Moving it with your foot is kicking it."

"No, it's not."

"Yes it is. Look, I'm not going to sit here and argue with you. You were *moving* the ball with your foot in the house. I've told you over and over you can't play soccer in the house."

"But I wasn't *playing*—"

"I don't care what you call it! You disobeyed me." I jumped to my feet, reached over, and yanked the ball out of his arms. "I'm taking this for a while. You'll have to earn it back."

"But it's not fair!"

"What's not fair is you lying to me and disobeying me."

"I'm not lying to you."

"Yes!" I began to pace, trying to contain my mounting anger. "You lied to me about not playing soccer in the house. You lied to me about. . ." I looked around, trying to remember the things he'd said that incensed me so much before ". . .about leaving the toilet seat up in the bathroom." My gaze continued to sweep the room. "And you lied to me about breaking that cross." I pointed to where the broken glass ornament had been hanging in the living room window.

"What? I didn't break it, I told you."

"I don't believe you anymore. You've lied too many times."

"No, you're—"

"Stop it! Just go to your room and stay there for the rest of the night."

"But we're going to Dad's tonight."

I could almost feel smoke coming out of my ears. If I told Jeff to punish Evan, he would likely buy him a new video game instead.

"Fine. But give me your iPod. You've just lost it for a week."

"That's not fair! You're blaming me for stuff I didn't do! You always blame me. You can't figure out what really happened so you're just blaming me. You're the worst investigator ever."

"Go get your iPod." I pointed upstairs, trying to keep my arm from shaking with the rage seething inside. "Now."

"No." He crossed his arms in front of his chest. "It's not fair."

"Okay, *I'm* going to get it, then. And now you won't get it back for a *month*." I stalked upstairs and found the iPod on the shelf next to his bed.

When I came back down, I made a great show of locking the iPod in the safe in the closet where I keep our birth certificates and savings bonds from Aunt Helen. Evan wasn't watching; he was lying facedown on the sofa.

"Go pack your stuff," I ordered. For once, I would actually look forward to seeing him ride off with Jeff for the weekend. I hated being so angry with him. He was my baby and I was supposed to protect and love him, not yell and punish and feel the urge to, well, not hurt him, but to do something Child Protective Services wouldn't approve of. That anger was scary. But most of all it was sad.

Without a word and without looking in my direction, Evan scrambled up the stairs. I didn't see him again until Jeff's car honked out front. He followed Alicia down the stairs, pointedly not looking in my direction.

"I bet Brian will love your nails," Alicia said as she gave me a hug. "You are going to see him tonight, right?"

"Maybe."

She gave me a stern, almost motherly look of disapproval. "Maybe? I thought you promised you would."

"And you would know that because—?"

She tapped her forehead. "I'm psychic."

I laughed. "Right. Have a good weekend."

"We will," she answered for both of them, quickly shooing Evan out the door.

It's funny how much my daughter understands. One minute she's acting like a surly twelve-year-old, the next minute she's my mom. I think I like it. I'm not sure.

When I opened the door to the hall at Brian's church, I was immediately hit with the sound of singing, and I was pretty sure it wasn't a serenade for me. It was two girls' voices, attempting to sing in harmony and failing rather spectacularly. When I got close enough to see them standing at the piano, I realized it was two of the three crabby candy canes. I'd forgotten they had a song; since they were never at practice, we always skipped it.

Well, they were at practice tonight. Now. Early. When I was supposed to have Brian all to myself.

Nobody was actually playing the piano; Brian hit a

key and then they'd start singing a cappella.

"What does it mean to give?" one girl belted out.

"Gi–iivve," the other echoed in a warbling style that I think was a deliberate imitation of some awful pop singer.

"Good!" Brian encouraged. "That's the whole message of this play, so you need to sing it loud."

"It would be better to sing it in tune," I murmured. "We can make it loud with microphones."

"Oh, hi, Karen." Brian turned toward me. "Did you say something?"

"No. No, don't let me interrupt you. Go right ahead. . ." *and ruin our date*, I added to myself, trying not to glare at the offending teenagers.

They repeated the phrase a few more times and then moved on to something about making time for Jesus at Christmas. Ha! Whoever wrote that line had no idea what an insane commercial rush the season had become. It really didn't have anything to do with Jesus anymore. Now it was all about deadlines. Presents to the relatives had to be mailed by this date. Presents for the teachers had to be ready by another date. Cookies for the Scout Christmas party had to be baked by that date. And practices for the Christmas play, well, they were apparently endless. No one had time for Jesus at Christmas, unless he lay quietly in his manger like a lifeless, plastic child.

I was already behind. I had nothing ready to send to my parents or two of my three aunts. The nieces and nephews just got gift cards, but I still had to remember to buy and mail them. Was I going to do Christmas cards this year? There were so many people I wanted to stay in touch with, and all year I kept promising myself that at least I'd write to them at Christmas.

And I really needed to clean or at least dust before I put up decorations. Most of my neighbors already had lights up. The kids were dying to get out the tree and decorate, but I just hadn't found the time yet. That's probably what I should have been doing now, getting the house straightened up and furniture moved so that there was room to stick a big fake evergreen tree in the middle of everything.

Instead, I was listening to the equivalent of nails on a chalkboard.

Other kids started arriving, so before too much longer, Brian moved away from the piano and told everyone to take their places for the start of the show. "We only have two more practices," he announced. "The next one will be a dress rehearsal. So I want everyone to do their best!"

I dug my copy of the script out of my handbag and waited to see how many parts I would have to read this time.

"What's wrong?" Brian came to sit down beside me at the back of the auditorium where I had retreated to rest with a handful of Cheetos and a Diet Coke while he made sure that each of the kids had a ride home.

"Why do you assume something's wrong?"

"I don't know. You just looked upset onstage. Unhappy. Distracted."

Bored was more like it. But I guess there was more to it than that. The fight with Evan still bothered me. Anger hung over me like a cloud. Except I wasn't really angry anymore. I was just depressed.

"It's been a long week," was what I finally decided to say. I didn't want to whine or bore him with complaints.

"Yes," he said as he nodded, "it looks that way." He leaned closer and lowered his voice. "But this week had the same number of days as the week before. So something must have happened to make it feel longer. Do you want to talk about it?"

"You're using your 'youth counselor' tone of voice," I warned.

"Sorry." He raked his hands through his hair.

"And you need a haircut," I observed to get the topic of conversation away from myself.

"Yeah, my Mom is still always onto me about that. She doesn't care whether it's historically accurate or not. She thinks I look like a hippie."

"No, not really." I gave him an appraising look. "A pirate, I think. And I didn't mean you needed to cut it short. You just need to cut off the split ends."

"Okay, Mom."

"I'm not your mom!" My voice came out more sharply than I'd intended.

He winced. "I was joking, you realize."

"I know."

"Are you having problems with the kids?"

"You're acting like a counselor again."

"No, I'm trying to act like a friend. What's bothering you?"

I sighed. "I guess you wouldn't believe me if I said I'd eaten too many Cheetos and was having a reaction to all the food coloring?"

"Nice try."

I leaned back in my chair and stared at my fake nails for a moment. "I guess I'm upset because I got so angry at Evan for lying to me this afternoon. It just, I don't know, kinda won't go away."

"Are you keeping it bottled up inside?"

I shook my head. "Oh no. I did the whole accusing-yelling-grounding Bad Mother Routine. No, I definitely didn't try to keep it inside. I probably let too much out."

He shrugged. "It happens. That doesn't make you a bad mother."

"Yes it does." I was failing at the one thing I thought I was good at. And it was tearing me apart. I felt the familiar lump rising in my throat again. "I should control my temper better. What kind of an example does that set?"

"I don't think you're really angry. I think you're really hurt."

"Maybe so," I sniffed. "I feel like I'm losing my little boy. I can't trust him anymore. And it's only going to get worse, when instead of worrying about lies about breaking things, I'll be worried about drugs and other stuff."

He wrapped his arm around my shoulder and I leaned back against him.

"If I wasn't so busy, if I had more time for him," I continued, trying to blink back tears, "he might be more honest with me. I think he's lashing out, trying to get attention to make up for my neglect."

"You do not neglect your son. I don't think I've ever met a mother who's more conscientious—"

"I'm spending a lot more time thinking about work, and then spending time with you. . ."

He leaned forward to look me in the face. "Karen, it's okay to have a life. You need to have one."

"I don't need to have so much of a life. I need to be there for my kids—the ones who need me."

"You don't have too much of a life."

"Well, of course you'd say that." I pulled forward, away from him. "You have too much yourself." *Leaving no time to be there for the one who needed him. Namely, me.*

And that, I suddenly realized, was a big part of the problem. I was feeling hurt and worried about my son, certainly. But I was also feeling hurt and resentful that Brian seemed to make time for everyone but me. Of course, he had time for me now. Was I being fair?

He was very quiet, and I assumed I had offended him.

"I'm sorry." I sat back again, but not leaning on him as I'd done before. "I have no right to make judgments about how you spend your time."

"Ah, well, I was thinking you may be right, actually." He clasped his hands together and stared at the seat in front of him. "When I realized that Chloe was gone, really gone, that I could talk to her but I would never hear her answer, then I couldn't stand being alone at home. I made sure I had something to do every minute. And I guess it's habit now."

"I can see that. I guess it's probably better to jump into too much life, than to withdraw from it completely, like I did when my marriage failed."

He pulled me close, enveloping me in warmth and strength. "I think maybe God put us together to help us work through this, to even our lives out."

As much as I enjoyed the sensation of Brian's embrace,

I couldn't help but stiffen. How did God get into the middle of this? God was worried about praying and going to church and, well, God stuff. Not relationship stuff. This was very human. We finally had time to ourselves, time when we really connected with each other. And now Brian had brought in God to join us, like having a chaperone on a date. It ruined the moment.

"There is a plan behind it all," he insisted, not letting me pull away. "Though we can't always see it."

Yeah, whatever, I wanted to say.

"Talking about God makes you uncomfortable," he observed.

"I guess."

"He's always there, you know. Whether you ask him to be or not. But he'll wait until you're ready."

A chaperone that would never leave. Great. That's all I need. A great big omnipotent chaperone who would make us keep six inches apart when we danced and would be there watching whenever we kissed, which we hadn't done as often as I'd wanted to. With the image of God hanging over me now, I didn't think I'd ever kiss Brian or any other man ever again. Though I still felt stiff and uncomfortable, Brian would not relax his hold around me. We sat still, not speaking, listening to the sound of rain dripping from the eaves outside. More rain. Evan would be wishing for snow. "I hate rain in December," I murmured, looking toward the windows that were too high up to reveal much of anything other than the dark sky.

"I think the rain is a comfort, knowing that God sends the water we need."

There He was again, the hovering chaperone.

"And the sound of water is so steady, like it can't be rushed," Brian continued in a low voice. "The rain will come in due season, not when we want it, but when we need it, washing the world clean."

I turned to look at him. "Now you sound like a poet."

"You inspire me."

"That was really bad." I shook my head. "Very cheesy."

"Sorry."

"Speaking of cheesy, I guess I should clean up the Cheetos." I started to stand up, but Brian pulled me back down. He's a lot stronger than I am, so just a gentle tug from him sent me flying back into his arms.

Or maybe that's just where I wanted to be, so I didn't need much encouragement.

"Don't go just yet." He stretched to the side to reach a light switch on the wall. Suddenly the room was enveloped in darkness, except for the lights on the stage at the far end. With the half-painted backdrop and miscellaneous props on the stage, I could almost picture the performance that would take place soon.

"A theater is never really empty, is it?" he said softly, as if he knew what I was thinking. We did understand each other a little. Maybe a lot. Maybe Brian wasn't so far off when he said God put us together. I relaxed back against him.

He kissed the back of my neck, and I was amazed at how a simple touch could be so soothing and yet so exciting at the same time. Warmth radiated from him. I turned and stretched up to kiss his chin. And then he leaned closer and we were kissing, like I'd wanted to for so long. With the rain dripping steadily outside and all the time in the world. And I didn't even care that God was watching.

14

On Monday morning, I decided my first priority was to find Craig Freels, even before I went into the office. So just before I got out of the van, I called to leave a message that I would be in later.

Since I had peeled off the fake nails before breakfast that morning, I was now able to make phone calls with ease. I remembered that I had a cell phone message I hadn't listened to yet. There were actually two messages, but one was just a reminder about a doctor's appointment. The other was Doreen, from Clipper Insurance.

"Hi, Karen. I know I told you the owners of the Blue Moon—what's their names—the Photosynthesis-Acropolis, whatever, you know who I mean—they hadn't filed any claims. But something new just showed up in the database. It's a claim filed by someone else, but it's a loss at the Blue Moon. So I'm going to look into it and see what I can find out." The voice paused while she took a breath.

I'll owe you one, Doreen.

"Then you'll owe me big time," her voice continued. "Talk to ya later."

I tried to return the call, but the switchboard wasn't open yet, so I ended up just leaving her a voicemail message in return. Then I flipped the phone shut and simply stared at the dusty dashboard for a while. I had become so certain that this case involved Freels somehow that I might have missed some clues about the owners' possible involvement.

I fought the urge to head immediately to the Blue Moon. For one thing, the store wouldn't open for over an hour. And I needed to finish what I started and check out Craig Freels. I started up the stairs to his apartment with brisk determination.

After I had knocked for about ten minutes, Robby finally pulled open the door, his eyes glazed half-shut with sleep.

"Is your brother home?" I didn't hold out much hope; if Craig was home, he was sleeping even more soundly than Robby had been.

He rubbed the light fluff of hair on his chin that was probably supposed to be a goatee. "Must be out walking Gypsy."

"The dog?" I guessed.

"Ferret. He takes her down to the woods around the trolley trail most mornings."

"Isn't he afraid she'll run away?"

He shook his head. "She's on a leash."

Okay, well, I guess artists have to do something to be eccentric. "Thanks. I'll go look for him there."

His face split into an enormous yawn.

I offered an apologetic smile. "Sorry to have come so early."

"'S okay." He took a swipe at the door to shut it and then turned away without waiting to see whether it actually did.

As I made my way carefully down the stairs strewn with rollerblades, rolled up newspapers, and coupons from the tops of pizza boxes, I wished Craig Freels had been a little lazier. Instead of tromping through the woods on a frigid December morning, it would be nice if I could head to the nearest bakery to look for him.

Rather than walking down the hill as Craig had surely done, I decided to drive down to the entrance to the trail, just on the other side of the river, and park in the convenient parking lot of the Old Mill Bakery. Of course, since I had used their parking facilities, I had to buy something, didn't I? I splurged on a latte and a mammoth pastry covered with cinnamon sugar. Then I headed past the silent Trolley Stop tavern and climbed the stone staircase that led up to the end of the hillside trail.

It was difficult to walk fast without spilling my coffee, but my pace improved after I accidentally dropped my pastry into a pile of muddy leaves. Well, there was a whole bunch of calories I didn't have to worry about.

I could see a couple hundred yards down the trail before it curved around through the woods. If Craig kept to the paved path, I should eventually spot him fairly easily.

Paved path? That didn't sound like something you'd walk a ferret on. He could be anywhere meandering through the hilly forest.

He probably liked to dress in dark, dull colors, too, so he would blend in with the barren winter trees and hillsides strewn with rocks and brown leaves. Should I just wait at the end of the trail? That would probably be the most logical thing to do. A good investigator had to be patient. Dave frequently spent hours waiting for suspects or witnesses.

But after a few minutes of pacing back and forth, watching my breath form clouds in the damp morning air, I decided I just wasn't a good investigator. I wanted to *do* something, not just wait for something to happen.

Robby had said Craig liked the river, so maybe he took his ferret down to the stream at the bottom of the hill. I knew the stream ran alongside the path for a while. Years ago when we used to take Alicia riding her little pink bike down the trail, she would freeze in fear when we reached that spot. She couldn't actually end up in the water unless she climbed off her bike, walked over to the edge of the path, and jumped. But she was terrified, and we usually had to push, carry, or drag her past that point in the trail.

Just the sort of place an artist obsessed with dead things might find appealing, right? I started toward it.

When I got to the spot where the ground on the left side of the trail dropped sharply, I looked down. There was the stream, just as I remembered. All I had to do was climb down the really steep slope without ruining my good work shoes.

Very soon shoe preservation was the last thing on my mind. I just wanted to get down to the stream without breaking my neck. I clung to saplings and vines as if I were on a controlled descent to the Amazon, trying to keep away from a school of half-starved piranhas. At last, my feet were on semi-level ground, and I heaved a big sigh of relief, looking longingly at the remainder of my coffee that sat abandoned in a dented cup on the bank above.

"It's easier getting back up, believe it or not."

I turned at the sound of the unexpected male voice.

It belonged to a young man with a wiry build and dark, unkempt hair. He nodded toward the stream. "Water's up.

And moving more than usual today, even sparkles when the sun breaks through the clouds."

Could it be. . .yes! There was a ferret tied to a tree on a long leather lead. This must be Craig Freels. And he seemed to be as talkative as his brother.

But would he stay that way if he knew I had come looking for him?

"This is one of my favorite places," I lied. Well, I had somewhat fond memories of Alicia attached to this spot, so maybe it wasn't actually a lie.

"Really?"

"Well, I usually just sit up at the top."

"Most people do. But you get a completely different perspective from down here." He waved toward a large, flat rock where he had spread out an open sketchbook, pencils, and a small camera with a lens that protruded from the front like a long snout. "Even a place to sit."

"What are you working on?" He couldn't find that question suspicious at all, could he? It would be natural for anyone to ask.

"Those trees, there." He nodded toward a clump of skinny tree trunks leaning on each other. Not surprisingly, they looked pretty dead, but that could have just been because it was winter.

"They need each other to stay up," he continued.

"So are you drawing them?"

He nodded. "And I took some pictures. Then when I get home, I'll superimpose the photo as a transparency over the sketch then highlight it with metallics."

"Wow!" I responded appreciatively, hoping he wouldn't be insulted by my next question. "Are you an art student or something?"

"Or something," he said with an embarrassed grin. "I dropped out."

"But why?" I waved toward the sketchbook. "You obviously have a lot of talent."

He shrugged. "It was time."

"Time? Like you'd been in school too long?" I wondered if his parents had tired of paying tuition.

"Yeah," he mused. "That's a good way to think of it."

"What do you mean?"

He sighed. "My favorite teacher—he'd been my advisor ever since I started—he, well, disappointed me. I decided it was time to move on."

Ooh, I needed to tread carefully here. I had a feeling he was referring to Tollefsen, and I needed to know what he'd done to "disappoint" his protégé. I had to encourage him to elaborate without seeming nosy.

Would I use the Brian/counselor method, putting on my gentlest voice to ask, *"How did he disappoint you?"*

Should I use the Brittany approach and, like a peer, simply repeat his words as if clueless to their meaning? *"Disappointed?"*

Or should I act like my kids and immediately suggest a scenario so obnoxious that he'd have to correct or affirm me? *"What, did he plant a bomb in the library or something?"*

In the end, my motherly instincts won out, I guess. The guy looked so sad that it was making me sad, too. "I'm sorry," was all I said.

And that encouraged him to continue.

"Yeah, I was sorry, too." Freels picked a brown leaf off a sapling and examined it for a moment before casting it to the ground. "He was a real expert, y'know? I could've learned a lot more from him."

"How long did you study with him?"

"Three years. About. It was at the end of my third year that he. . ."

I held my breath, but decided not to say anything, even though my mind was screaming, *"He what?"*

He sighed. "I guess I should be flattered, really."

Now *that* I could ask about. "Flattered?"

"He copied one of my paintings. An assignment he'd given me for studio class."

I felt my mouth gape open. "He copied your work? Isn't that illegal?"

"That's what my girlfriend thought. But he didn't exactly copy my specific work. He just copied my idea."

"Well, no wonder you quit. You must have been really mad."

"I expected better of him," he said softly, staring down at the pebbles lining the edge of the stream.

"Did you sue him?"

"What is it with women and lawsuits?" he asked with disgust. "No, I didn't sue him. It wasn't like he hit me with his car or anything." His voice returned to its earlier sense of sad calm. "He just destroyed my trust and lost all my respect. You don't sue someone for that."

Wow. This kid had a maturity that most of us never even strive for. The concepts of trust and respect are just empty words to most of us, an old-fashioned saying with no place in modern life.

"So you don't. . .hate him?" I asked at last.

He shook his head. "No. I feel sorry for him."

Okay, so Vicki wasn't damaging Tollefsen's paintings to get even. Craig Freels plainly had no desire for revenge, so if Vicki wanted to get back into his good graces, she wouldn't make a move against Tollefsen.

Would she?

Maybe she didn't understand or accept Craig's wishes. Robby said Craig had been trying to break things off for a long time, and she hadn't let go.

I needed to know more about the Vicki that Craig knew, not the pert and perky flight attendant Vicki that I saw at the Blue Moon.

"But your girlfriend wanted you to sue?" I prompted.

"Yeah." His lip curled in disgust.

Now maybe I could get him to open up about Vicki the way he'd opened up about Tollefsen.

I smiled encouragingly. "So I take it she's not your girlfriend any longer?"

"No."

I waited, hoping he'd continue on as he'd done earlier, but now he just stared morosely at the water.

"I'm sorry," I said again. But the words didn't have the magic effect they'd had earlier, maybe because I wasn't really sorry this time. I was starting to think of Vicki, nice as she was, as a little spoiled and shallow, used to throwing temper tantrums when something upset her. Craig Freels deserved better, from what I could tell. I wasn't sorry they had broken up. Moreover, this time I hadn't expressed sorrow out of a true feeling of empathy, but rather in the self-serving hope that I could encourage Craig to spill some dirt about his ex-girlfriend.

It wasn't working.

"Gypsy is getting restless," he said abruptly. "We're going to move on."

He untied the ferret, picked up his camera, closed up his sketchpad, and shoved his pencils into his jacket pocket.

"Okay, well, uh, nice talking to you."

"Yeah, same here." But he didn't look at me, and I had the distinct impression that while he might have enjoyed talking to me at first, he'd now rather forget our conversation entirely.

—

My coffee was cold by the time I pulled myself up the stream bank back up to the trail. I dumped the rest of it into what I hoped wasn't poison ivy (the last thing this world needs is poisonous weeds on caffeine). Then I walked back to the car quickly, not realizing how chilled I'd gotten standing in the cold mud down by the water. And since I had no idea where Rodney might have hidden the coffeemaker this week, I decided to grab another cup at the bakery before I drove back to the office.

A strange, metallic sound met my ears as I walked up the stairs to DS Investigations. I opened the door to see Rodney sitting on the floor in front of Brittany's desk. He was holding up a string of long metal tubes—chimes, I guess—and tapping them softly with a wooden mallet. Incense burned in small blue lacquered trays on either end of the desk.

His eyes were closed and he looked serene, but every few seconds his forehead would twitch as if he remembered where he was.

"Er, hi, Rodney." I didn't want to interrupt, but it seemed rude to walk right past him without saying anything.

A frowning Dave peered out of his office. "Oh, you're finally here."

"Good morning to you, too." I stuck out my tongue. "I called and left a message to tell Rodney that I was working on assignment and would be in late. And I'm not even that late. So don't give me that look."

"We have a problem."

I glanced around at the stacks of files and loose papers heaped in various places throughout the office. "Yeah, it looks that way. I guess maximizing an office can be a painful process."

Dave stepped closer and lowered his voice. "I still can't find the coffeepot. I'm beginning to think he hid it deliberately."

"You should be drinking tea," Rodney called over, still with his eyes closed. "It cleanses the system. And besides, it is much more fashionable and gives the office an up-to-date flair."

Brittany came out of the kitchen rolling her eyes.

"You see what I mean?" Dave insisted.

"Oh, I know." This was what I'd warned him about only last week. "What's he doing with the doorbell?" I whispered.

"The, uh. . ." Dave held up his hands, pantomiming Rodney's gestures with the chimes. "I have no—he told me, but I forgot."

Brittany came over. "I think he said he was cleansing the old energies from the room."

"More funk spray, right?"

She nodded.

"How long has he been like this?"

Dave shrugged. "I dunno. He got really ticked when I moved some coins that were in some sort of magical red envelope."

Rodney's eyes snapped open. "You spent the Coins of Prosperity on a hot dog," he huffed indignantly before closing his eyes again.

"Well I can't very well be prosperous on an empty stomach," Dave hurtled back.

I walked toward the stacks of paper and turned to address Dave. "So did he just pull out half the files and then stop? Don't do that!" I said as I saw Dave take aim at Rodney with a potato chip lid.

"He hates these things," Dave muttered as he reluctantly tucked the lid into his shirt pocket.

"You placed too many red cans in close proximity," Rodney called over to us, obviously listening, though pretending not to. "It created a preponderance of red in one place, infusing the energy with anger and agitation."

Well, certainly Rodney was looking a little angry and agitated.

"How about if we agree to remove the potato chips if he gives us the coffeepot?" I suggested to Dave. "Sort of an exchange of prisoners."

"It's worth a shot," he said hopefully.

This couldn't continue. If Dave wasn't going to face the reality of what "his" business had become, I would force him to see it. "Dave." I grabbed his arm. "Come here for a minute." I pulled him into his office. Brittany looked like she wanted to join us, but I waved her away. "Okay,"

I said when I had shut the door firmly. "I understand that we need someone else to help with administrative stuff, since I'm out more and Brittany is about as efficient as a government employee."

"That's really low. I'm surprised at you."

"You know it's true. So we need someone, but Rodney just isn't working out. His. . .style just isn't right for us."

He pursed his lips. "I think you're right."

"So can you find a nice way to let him go? We'll find someone else without too much trouble."

"I think we have to give him a little more time."

I sighed in frustration. "How much time do you want to give him? How long are you willing to pay the guy to wave smoke and bang on chimes?"

"He has some good ideas."

"And some really lousy ones."

"We just need to make him understand."

I shook my head. "No, we don't. We just need an employee who can take direction from the bosses. Don't look at me like that."

"This is *my* firm, Karen. Don't try to give me that 'I'm the big sister and I know what's best' speech. There's only one boss around here and it's me."

I took a step back, feeling almost as if he had punched me in the gut like he used to do when we were kids.

That hurt. He didn't trust me, after all the years we'd worked together. I meant no more to the business than a clueless college intern like Brittany.

"You just don't like Rodney because *I* hired him," Dave continued, his voice rising. "You think anyone *you* hired would be better."

"That's not true," I said quickly. Actually it was true, but that's only because Dave had no idea what it took to run an office. I really did know what was best, and he just didn't want to acknowledge it.

And he didn't have to, because he was the one making all the money and paying the salaries. He was "the boss."

Without another word, I turned and stalked out of his office.

15

Brian wasn't home when I called him that night, so I left a generic message and really hoped he'd call me back. He was right about me feeling hurt by Evan's behavior, and now I had Dave being obnoxious, too. Making me feel worthless because he held the power of the paycheck over me. Didn't my years of service count for anything? Wasn't my experience worth something? Shouldn't he at least consider my opinion?

All I could do was try to wrap up the Blue Moon assignment as quickly as possible. That would show him. I knew there had to be a connection between Vicki, Craig, and the damage to the paintings. But nothing made sense, and there was certainly nothing I could prove. I needed to get Vicki to admit to something.

When I came into the Blue Moon on Tuesday, I brought a big basket of warm blueberry muffins. I figured this would put everyone in a good mood, and it certainly worked for Eric. He ate four, praised them profusely, and then bought a little china saucer from the Odds and Ends box so he could present Vicki with a blueberry muffin on a blue plate.

His devotion to Vicki was getting hard to watch. I was sure Vicki had talked him into damaging merchandise for her. Yet behind his back, she made no secret of her contempt for him.

"Thank you!" she gushed, giving him a quick kiss on the cheek. "You're such a sweetie."

I really hoped she wouldn't ask him to do anything else illegal for her, or that if she did, he would have the sense to say "no."

When Mrs. P. came in, I was happy to have a treat to offer her, since she was always bringing in things for us. But she didn't smile when I held up the basket.

"I'm missing my husband," she announced as soon as she saw me. Her mouth settled into a stern line.

"Oh, Mr. P.'s in the back," Vicki assured her.

"I know where he is," she said sternly. "But he should be at home, drinking coffee and reading the paper. Not living in his store like a homeless man."

Homeless people usually did not own business establishments, but I got the point. Her husband had been stuck guarding the store for too long. "How about if I take one of these back to the office for you," I offered. That would give her the chance to rail at me in private.

"Yes, thank you." She turned and plodded back toward the office, her heavy tote bags crinkling with each step.

I followed a few minutes later, after turning my cell phone to vibrate so Brittany couldn't interrupt me with inane questions. Mrs. P. had reached the breaking point, but if I could just make her understand how close I was to making the case, then she might be able to hang on a little longer.

"So I think we should fire her," Mrs. P. announced to her husband as I walked in and shut the door. Though she was speaking to him, from the look that she gave me right afterward it was obvious that she meant for me to hear.

Mr. P. shrugged. "We haven't had any more damage lately."

"That's because you've been staying here." Did I really say that? I guess I was just trying to beat Mrs. P. to the obvious.

She looked a little flabbergasted. "Uh, yeah. That's exactly right."

"Look," I pleaded as I came closer. "I know this is not an ideal situation—"

"Ideal!" She huffed indignantly. "It's like we're not even married anymore. How would you feel if your husband slept someplace else every night?"

"He does," I said calmly. "He sleeps at my best friend's house. We're divorced now. And I have a new best friend."

Actually, I didn't really, but that was beside the point. I would find a new best friend sometime.

Maybe Brian was becoming my new best friend?

All of this had nothing to do with the case.

"What I was trying to say," I continued, trying to figure out just how to convince her, "is that I think I know where the damage is coming from, but I need proof." Again I wondered whether I should tell them about Eric's confession. But I had to wait until I knew for certain what the insurance claim involved.

"You've had lots of time to get proof," Mrs. P. insisted. "We've paid your firm plenty to get proof. If we operated the way you do, we'd be closed in a month."

"Maybe there's someone else in the firm who's. . . more experienced at getting the proof you need?" Mr. P. suggested.

Ouch. I swallowed hard. "If we brought in someone else," I explained, "we'd have to start virtually all over to gain your employees' trust. It's more likely we'll get a confession rather than physical evidence, so trust is key."

"Start over?" Mrs. P. shook her head. "Oh, no. You've taken too much of our money already."

"Please just give me a little more time," I pleaded, the lump in my throat growing larger. I don't think Dave ever had to beg his clients for anything.

"We'll think it over," Mr. P. said reassuringly. "Now why don't you get back and work on the trust issue, like you said."

"Okay." I sniffed back tears, embarrassed that I had let myself show so much weakness. I hurried from the office, hoping I still had a pack of tissues in my purse.

"What's the matter?" Vicki asked as I made a dive for my purse in the bottom drawer behind the counter. Vicki was at the counter sorting through a box of keys, trying to unlock a lacquered jewelry box.

I was struck with sudden inspiration. "Boyfriend," I said, giving full rein to the misery I was feeling. This topic had garnered sympathy from Brittany, so it probably would with Vicki, too. "He can be so. . .I don't know. . . so wrong." There, that should work. Vicki must surely feel that Craig was wrong in trying to end things between them.

"Oh, I'm sorry to hear that. Hey, thanks for bringing in the muffins, they were a big hit. I won't need to eat lunch now."

That's it? That's all the sympathy I got? And no opening to ask about her love life, either. But that wouldn't stop me from trying. "Don't you think men can be impossible sometimes?" I asked.

"They can be. There's so much they don't understand."

She favored me with a sympathetic smile. "Don't worry. Whatever it is, I'm sure he'll come around eventually. It takes guys awhile to understand even really obvious things."

"Patience is not one of my strengths," I admitted, truthfully enough.

"You know how when you were little your parents would say something like, 'I'm doing this for your own good,' and you didn't believe them? Well it's like that with guys. You just have to stand your ground and wait until they realize that you know what's best."

Boy, did that sound condescending. I mean, I guess I agreed with her pretty much, but it sure sounded obnoxious.

And I'm not even sure it's true, really, because I wouldn't say I always knew "what's best" any better than Brian did. And as for my disagreement with Dave, I'm sure he knew "what's best" for handling the discouraged clients and finessing a confession. No, I definitely did not always know what's best.

Dave's voice echoed in my head. *"Don't try to give me that 'I'm the big sister and I know what's best' speech."* I'll bet I sounded as condescending then as Vicki did just now.

"Yeah, I guess you're right," I finally said, more to keep her talking than because I believed she was right. "What's the most annoying thing your boyfriend's ever done?"

She grinned shyly. "Oh, I don't know."

"C'mon, I'm sure you have a list. I dated a guy once who picked his teeth with his credit card when he was waiting to pay for something." I was married to him, actually, but I didn't think Vicki would relate well to that.

"Eew." She laughed. "I don't think I have anything that gross."

"It doesn't have to be gross," I insisted. *Just tell me something about Craig.*

"My boyfriend has a really annoying brother," she said tentatively.

"Okay, that's something."

"He's always there. He never leaves the apartment. He has no life whatsoever."

"What, does he play video games all day?"

"Yes, exactly. It's like living at Chuck E. Cheese's, with overgrown children and electronic shooting noises all day." She waved a key in the air to illustrate.

"Did you live with him?"

"Oh, no. Just visiting them was almost more than I could handle. We had to go out a lot. I couldn't stand being in the apartment."

Past tense. Should I mention it? I decided to try. "You said you couldn't stand it. Does that mean the brother finally moved out?"

She dropped the key with a dull thud. "No."

"Oh." I mustered all the sympathy I could. "I guess that means you guys aren't together anymore."

"We are, it's just that we're not together as much for a while. Just to give him some time."

Until he sees things your way. She looked a little forlorn, picking through the box of loose keys, and I decided it would be cruel to push her anymore in that direction. I knew she was referring to Craig and that she was expecting their relationship to continue.

"I do so much for him and he just doesn't see it," she said very softly, still looking down, her eyes glassy with tears.

I could almost feel sorry for her.

Then I heard a hand truck rumble in the back and saw Eric marching toward us with a big grin. There on the truck was the ceramic frog Vicki called "Cedric," and he was sitting on something that looked like a gold papier-mâché throne.

"Oh, how cute," she gushed. "Why don't you put our frog prince over there?" She pointed to a desk in the corner.

This guy obviously liked her a lot, and she had taken advantage of him, persuading him to damage merchandise for her.

And she'd taken advantage of her employers, too, damaging their goods for her own purpose. But what was that purpose?

She'd once said that Craig Freels was much better than Tollefsen. Did she think she could help foster Craig's reputation by damaging Tollefsen's work? That made no sense. She might sabotage a review of Tollefsen's paintings, but damaging the pictures themselves only hurt the owner of them.

Maybe she didn't see it that way. I glanced up at the damaged Tollefsen painting that was still hanging up high on the opposite wall. "Shouldn't we take that down and put up something else? Who's going to want to buy a painting with a cut in it?"

Vicki nodded. "That's what I said to Mrs. P. But she says a buyer might be interested in making the repair."

"But don't we have other inventory we could put up that might have a better chance of selling?"

"Actually, no, not at the moment. But we could buy more. There are a lot of talented local artists other than

Tollefsen, and we could promote them."

Should I suggest Freels? Or see if she did?

"Who would you recommend?"

"Oh, I don't know. We have a list somewhere."

Come on, Vicki. You can do better than that. "Didn't you mention once that Craig Freels was local?"

"Did I? Now that I think of it, I guess he is. And Geraldine Miller."

"Have you ever met either of them?"

"Of course."

I held my breath. *Tell me more!*

She didn't say anything else.

"So what are they like?" I prompted. "I've heard artists can be really weird."

There. I insulted her man. She should immediately come to his defense.

"Well," she said slowly, "I've heard that Geraldine lives with a whole house full of parrots. She talks to them all day long while she paints."

That would explain why her paintings were so bad. She was distracted by a running conversation about crackers and other parrot concerns. "Does Freels have any weird pets?"

"I. . .don't know."

Okay, she was lying. Anyone who had spent any time in that apartment could not help but notice the smell of ferret.

"Does he dress weird?" I continued. "Wear a beret or anything?"

She shrugged. "Define *weird*. I mean, with some of the hippie tie-dye shops we have on this street, you could say half the town dresses weird."

"True." I was going to have to lay off soon or she would realize my questioning was deliberate. But I tried one more time. "I'll bet he was young, if he was a student of Tollefsen's. Did you think he was cute?"

"You don't have to be young to be a student."

I gave up. She was showing signs of extreme caution but no guilt. Questioning her further would only make her suspicious.

Guilt might convince someone else to be more forthcoming with his answers. I grabbed the dust mop and went to look for Eric.

As I was "cleaning" in the back room where Eric made repairs, Mr. P. came up behind me and cleared his throat.

"Uh-ahem. Karen, when you have time, could you come over to the office? Mrs. P. wants to talk to you."

"Should I go right now?"

"Uh, you can finish what you're doing, if you want."

I had a feeling this was going to be unpleasant. Like when I tell my kids I want to talk to them. I'm not usually getting ready to tell them what a good job they've done folding laundry. So I decided to dust, that is, to look for Eric a little more first.

He came in from the back just as I thought I was going to have to go out and pretend to dust the alley.

"Hi." I waved the handle of the dust mop.

He nodded in return. "Hey, Karen." Then his attention went immediately back to the lamp base in his hand.

"What are you working on today?"

"Oh, this lamp needs rewiring."

"Wow." I decided to try flattering him to see if I could get him to relax a little. My first thought had been to threaten to expose his involvement in the damaged antiques if he didn't reveal who else was involved. But if he had done it for Vicki, he wasn't going to turn in the woman he adored. So I went with flattery instead. "I think I'd be afraid to touch the wiring. Can't you get electrocuted or something?"

"Not when it's unplugged."

"I mean when you plug it back in to test it."

"I'll put in new wiring. It's not that big a deal."

"I still wouldn't want to do it."

My flattery seemed to be working. Eric stopped and stood in front of me as if he was getting ready to speak.

I smiled encouragingly. "Did you want to tell me something?"

"Well, I need to get to the drawers."

"Oh." I hadn't noticed that I had stopped dusting right in front of a bank of small drawers that looked like an old library card catalog.

So much for flattery. It was time to use guilt. "You know, Eric," I said slowly, refusing to relinquish my position in front of the drawers, "Mr. P. is stuck having to spend every night in this store until they put an end to the damage that's been happening around here."

His face grew as red as the truck in the fire station museum across the street. "I told you I promised not to damage anything else. Since insurance isn't covering anything."

"But won't you tell me why you damaged things in the first place? How do I know you won't change your mind?"

"I just won't, that's all."

"What made you do it?"

He looked away miserably. "I don't know."

"I don't think you did it for fun," I said softly.

"No."

"Did someone ask you to?"

"No!"

"Are you sure? If someone else wanted to damage things in the store, he or she might continue even if you stop. And then what will happen to Mr. and Mrs. P?"

"I don't think she'll—" He stopped himself and clutched the lamp base with both hands.

"Who?"

"No one."

"This wasn't your idea."

"Y–yes it was. And I said it was over, so you don't need to worry about it. You'll see. When Mr. P. realizes that nothing else is getting damaged, he'll be okay."

Sweat beaded on his forehead, which was furrowed in concentration. He was trying to convince himself as much as me. And probably succeeding. I wasn't going to get him to give me anything I could use. At least I got him to admit there was a "she" involved. So I finally let him get to the drawers full of nuts, bolts, and lamp wiring supplies.

"I hope you're right," I said as I headed toward the door. "Mrs. P. said she feels like they aren't even married anymore." *Guilt guilt guilt.* I hoped it would work its magic overnight.

My work here was done. At least for now. I stowed the dust mop behind the door and headed for the office.

"I think this should cover your fees through the end

of today," Mrs. P. said as I walked in.

"Huh?" I blinked stupidly and realized that she was holding a check out toward me.

"We've decided that we no longer need your services, but we will pay you for the work you've done so far of course. Such as it is."

"Thanks," I said automatically as I took the check. The reality was only now sinking in. I was fired. She fired our firm from the job because I had failed. A gaping pit seemed to open in the floor between me and her desk. "I'm really sorry. . ." I didn't finish.

I'm sorry I couldn't work faster. I'm sorry I couldn't get the confession you need to win a lawsuit. No court would believe the flimsy motive I had without a confession.

I'm sorry you didn't give me enough time. I'm sorry that I've let the firm down. I'm sorry that I failed as an investigator. I'm sorry that I'll be stuck in the office again now.

I'm sorry you gave up on me.

The pit of sadness began to fill with a sense of frustration. And anger.

"I'll send you a report detailing all that I've learned," I said curtly. Just as I was about to tell her that I knew who was responsible for the damage, I stopped myself. Mrs. P. wouldn't wait until I did this properly. She thought she knew best. And so I'd penalize her. Oh, I'd tell her what I knew, all right. I owed her that much. But she'd have to wait until I typed up a formal report. Which I would do when I had time. Maybe I'd get around to it next week.

Not until after Doreen found out what the insurance claim was about. I had to be sure they weren't using our firm to bolster their claim for insurance money.

"I'm sorry, too." Her mouth sank into that flat line again. She was sorry she had hired me.

"Uh, Mrs. Maxwell," Mr. P. added in a scratchy voice, his gaze focused on his hands. "If you want to go ahead and go now, you can. You don't have to wait until closing time today."

"If I leave suddenly, the employees will know something's up. I think it's better if I find a plausible reason to quit this afternoon."

"Oh, okay." He shrugged. "You know best."

His wife shot him a look as if to say that obviously wasn't true.

As I walked out of the office, I pulled my cell phone out. I would pretend to have a problem at home that forced me to quit. Then Vicki wouldn't get suspicious. When she received my report, Mrs. P. could confront her and maybe bully her into a confession.

The rush of anger that had buoyed me up during my confrontation with Mrs. P. ebbed away as I walked through the store. This could have been my second success.

I blinked to keep tears out of my eyes.

"Are you okay?" Vicki asked as I approached the counter.

"No," I sniffed. Should I say my daughter was sick and I needed to stay home and take care of her? No, that was overdoing it. "My dog is sick. Really sick. The vet thinks she has cancer." Now I could let the tears flow. The dog Dave and I had had as kids died of cancer when I was about ten. It had been sudden and sad.

"Oh, I'm so sorry." Vicki reached out to give me a hug, but it was one of those fake hugs where you don't really touch the other person.

"She's home alone all day while I'm working, and I didn't realize how bad she'd gotten. She hasn't been eating, and this morning I finally took her in to the vet. I just called to see how the tests came out." I shook my head. Were my tears for my failure at the Blue Moon? The humiliation I would feel in front of Dave, Rodney, and Brittany? The fears about my children? Or was I still mourning the loss of my first dog? It was probably a little of everything.

"I think I need to stay home with her, take care of her." *Be there for her the way I haven't been for my kids lately.*

"Oh, yes, I think so," Vicki agreed.

"Do you think Mr. P. will mind if I quit suddenly?"

"He won't. Mrs. P. might be annoyed, but I'll put in a good word for you. Besides, if you quit, what does it matter if she's mad at you?"

I glanced at my watch. Forty-five more minutes. That's when I'd leave. I wasn't going to run out with my tail between my legs. I would work until the store closed. Then I'd walk out with my head held high. After all, I had discovered the culprit. And when they received my report, Mr. and Mrs. P. might even be satisfied that it was enough.

I was not.

16

If I thought my mood was bad when I got home, that of my kids was even worse. Evan sulked when I wouldn't give him back his favorite soccer ball and Alicia was having a fight with what I had to assume was now her former BFF, Jennifer. In between yelling at the phone, hanging up the phone, and refusing to answer the phone when it rang again, she yelled at me for not buying her a cell phone. I was pretty sick of the sound of her voice long before dinner, and we all ate our Hamburger Helper in complete silence. Well, there was no talking, but there was no peaceful silence either because the dog was scratching almost constantly at the glass door, begging to come in so she could then beg at the dinner table.

"Forget it, Tara," I muttered through clenched teeth. "You're not coming in."

Alicia fixed me with a withering gaze of disdain. "She can't hear you, you know."

"Yeah, Mom," Evan added.

"I don't appreciate you taking that tone of voice with me, either of you."

"Well," Alicia said as she twirled her fork through a big blob of pasta on her plate "I don't appreciate listening to you talk to an animal over and over when she can't even hear you."

Evan sat back from the table and crossed his arms in front of his chest. "And I don't appreciate you taking my soccer ball when I'm supposed to practice."

"You should have thought of that before you broke the rule about kicking the ball in the house."

His scowl deepened. "I didn't kick the ball, I told you!"

"And you didn't leave clothes on the bathroom floor and you didn't break my crystal cross, either."

"Right."

"Well the ball was kicked—I was there, remember—and your clothes from yesterday are still lying on the bathroom floor, and I can't trust you anymore. Not at all."

"I picked up my clothes. Really. I did."

Without another word, I pushed back from the table, marched over to the bathroom near the front door, picked up the sweatpants and jacket that Evan had left the previous night, came back to the table, and dropped them in his lap.

"Alicia did it to make me look bad."

"And she broke the cross to make you look bad, too?"

"Probably."

She made a face at him. "I did not, twerp."

I waved her to be quiet.

"I'm sure she didn't. And I can't stand the fact that you're lying to me. I guess losing the iPod wasn't enough. You're grounded."

"It's not fair!"

I knew how the rest of the dialogue would play out so I barely listened as Evan ranted about my unfairness while I cleared the table and did the dishes. Really he should have been clearing the table, but I didn't want to argue about that, too.

After he had gone up to his room, the kitchen seemed very quiet. Too quiet. Now I had too much time to think about everything that was going wrong. I considered calling Brian, but I didn't want to talk, and besides, we'd probably just play phone tag like we had all week.

I ended up sitting down in front of the television with a big bowl of mint chocolate chip ice cream, watching some show where wives who suspect their husbands are cheating set up hidden cameras all around and everyone in the town watches the action on a bank of closed-circuit cameras set up at the local Dairy Queen.

Boy, if that show had been around when I was still married. . .ah, well, Ellicott City doesn't even have a Dairy Queen.

Anyway, with the help of reality TV, I managed to get through the rest of the night without thinking about the reality of my humiliation at being fired from the Blue Moon assignment. But I knew when I showed up at the office the next morning, on a morning when I normally would have been at the Blue Moon, I was going to have to explain everything to Dave right off the bat.

The morning got off to a rough start. Not only could I not park in my usual space, I couldn't park in any of the other spaces I'd been using lately. I had to park all the way up on Main Street and let the wind blow me down the icy sidewalk. Well, I tried to sort of skate down the sidewalk, but my balance isn't good enough, so I ended up walking in the slushy street. Big soggy red bows drooped from the lampposts, looking about as full of Christmas cheer as I felt.

When I reached the door to the building, two girls near Brittany's age were standing outside, rubbing their hands to keep warm.

"Can I help you?" I asked as I pulled out my keys.

"Rodney told us to report at 8:45," one of them answered, strands of long dark hair blowing in her eyes. "We're temps."

I managed to unlock the outside door with only a little jiggling of the handle. "I guess he's not here yet. Why don't you come on up and wait for him?"

While I wasn't sure why they had been told to "report," there was no sense making them wait out on an icy porch.

Their boots clip-clopped up the stairs behind me. When I unlocked and opened the door, I held my breath as I reached over to flip the light switch. Last time I was in the office, it was covered with stacks of file folders. How would it look now?

I couldn't tell immediately because the first thing I saw was two big boxes with pictures of inkjet printers on them.

"Well, at least we know where the scanners are," the dark-haired girl said to her companion.

"Scanners?" I looked at the boxes again and sure enough, they were all-in-one combination printer/scanner devices that could probably make coffee, too, if I just bought the right attachments. "Did Rodney ask you to come in to scan something?" Brittany knew how to scan documents, so why would he bring in two temps?

And not just two temps, but two new scanners. How much stuff was he planning to scan?

As I looked around at the piles of paper and file folders stacked all around the office, I started to feel a little queasy.

The nauseous feeling only worsened when I heard the brisk tap of Rodney's loafers coming up the stairs. "Good morning, Mrs. Maxwell," he said as he opened the door.

"And you must be Miss Hoffman and Miss Zelonky." He bowed to each of us in turn, which made the girls giggle.

Setting down a paper cup from Bean Hollow (which had better contain tea rather than coffee, since he insisted we should all be drinking tea), he carefully hung his overcoat on the coatrack, straightened his shirt collar and tie, and smoothed some imaginary wrinkles out of his suit jacket. Then he turned back to face us. "Mrs. Maxwell, why don't you show our temporary associates where to store their handbags while I set up the equipment?"

Should I object? Whatever he was doing was bound to be expensive and disruptive. But it was Dave's place to object, not mine.

"Come on, girls." I waved for them to follow me toward the kitchen. "And please call me Karen. Only despicable people like divorce attorneys call me 'Mrs. Maxwell.'"

I showed them a small cabinet where they could lock up their purses if they wanted to. "I'm afraid aliens have abducted our coffeemaker, but if you guys want coffee, I can run out and get some."

"That would be great," the dark-haired girl gushed effusively. "But I can get coffee for everyone if you tell me where to go."

"Deal. And you are. . .Miss Hoffman?" I reached out to shake her hand.

"Andrea Zelonky."

"I'm Julie Hoffman," the other girl said hoarsely, clutching at her throat. "Sorry, I have a cold."

"Right, I won't come near you, then." Despite my anxiety about seeing Dave and my worries about Rodney's latest plan, I found my mood improving just talking to these two young women. They both seemed so much more businesslike and confident than Brittany. Why couldn't Dave have hired someone like them as our intern?

As we walked out into the main part of the office so I could point Andrea in the right direction, I studiously ignored Rodney's struggles to remove a new printer/scanner from its Styrofoam and cardboard tomb. If he wanted help, he'd have to ask for it.

He was still struggling about ten minutes later when Brittany came in. "Maybe you have the box pointed in the wrong direction," she suggested.

"I'm sorry?" Rodney asked, panting with exertion.

"If you're using it to make money," she explained, "don't you need to point it east or something?"

I snickered at this unexpected little jab at Rodney's funk spray techniques. "Nice one," I said softly to Brittany as she came over to hang up her coat.

"Thank you," she whispered. "He's driving me crazy, too."

"Did you know he hired temps to do scanning?" I asked.

"Yeah, it's going to take a long time to put all the files in electronic format."

"What? He's planning to scan everything?"

"He says we should be a paperless office."

"And Dave agreed to this?" Dave, who scribbled down important information on the backs of old envelopes and who only used his computer to watch music videos?

"I guess," she answered, looking uneasy. "I don't think he understands what it means. Rodney says we can get rid of all the file cabinets. But if all our records are on computer, what happens if the computers break?"

"Good point." I was surprised she'd thought of it, actually.

"I don't think he's an expert on computers." She nodded toward Rodney, who was staring at the back of a scanner and muttering that he'd never be able to find the USB port.

"I'll talk to Dave about it," I promised.

"Thanks." She flashed me a smile, a real smile. I think maybe it was the first one I'd seen all day.

Like the watched pot that never boils, the watched door seemed like it would never open. When Dave came in, there would be so much to say. But if he'd been out on night surveillance, he might not be in until well after lunch. I'd probably explode by then.

I worked on some payroll tax forms that weren't even due yet, just to keep my mind off the upcoming confession about the case and confrontation about Rodney. Then right after the UPS guy (who was wearing a Santa hat with his shorts) dropped off some packages, Dave finally arrived.

"Hey everyone," he announced jovially, "it's snowing out. And since we've got such a big group today, we have enough people for a snowball fight. So put it on your schedule for 3:00."

The girls all laughed.

I glanced outside and saw one lone flurry drift past the window. "I'm in, even though I think it will be a snowflake fight, rather than snowballs." I lowered my voice. "But I need to talk to you about a few things first."

He tossed his jacket at the coatrack, where it caught the armhole, hanging firmly if unevenly. With a smile of satisfaction, he turned to face me. "Shoot."

"Can we go into your office?" I whispered.

"Yeah, uh, but let me first. . ." his gaze strayed to

where the coffeemaker used to be in the kitchen before he sighed and turned back to me. "Never mind. Um, sure, let's go." He waved for me to precede him.

I had to hurry before my resolve turned to mush. I wanted to make my announcement about the Blue Moon as businesslike as possible. I could apologize for my poor performance, but I would not whine or cry about it. Nor would I excuse it. I had tried my best.

And failed. I walked even faster, rushed headlong into Dave's office, and had to swerve to keep from banging into the desk.

"The Blue Moon case is over," I announced as soon as he'd closed the door.

"Great," he said, obviously startled. "You know who did it?"

"Yes." *But. . .*

"And you got him to confess?"

"Sort of."

He frowned. "Sort of? Unless you've got indisputable proof, then I wouldn't say the case is over until—"

I held up my hand to interrupt. "The case is over because we got fired. I got fired."

"You. . ."

"Got fired, yes. The clients thought I was taking too long. They handed me a check and called it quits."

"But did you tell them how close you were? I thought you had a confession."

"I did."

"And they weren't impressed?"

"I didn't tell them."

"Well, why the—" He raked his hand across his face. "Why not?"

I almost hated to say it. "There's a chance you might be right. The owners might be doing something to get insurance money after all." I had figured Eric was covering for Vicki when he refused to tell me who wanted him to damage the antiques. But the "she" he referred to could easily have been Mrs. P.

For once, Dave was near-speechless. "Really," he said at last. "Huh."

"Doreen found a new claim that mentions damage at the Blue Moon. The Photopouloses aren't listed as the claimants, however, so she's checking to see if she can get more information. Until I hear back from her, I didn't want to tell them anything."

He nodded. "Makes sense."

"I thought so."

"Especially since now if they file a claim, the owners can tell their insurer that they hired an investigator to find the culprit and they found nothing."

"But if Doreen tells me this claim isn't related, then I think with a little more work I can—"

Dave held up his hand to interrupt. "Whoa. We're off the clock now."

"Oh. Right."

The scope of work we do for clients is based on what they're willing to pay for. And the Photopouloses weren't paying for anything any longer. So this was it.

If the insurance angle looked fishy, I'd inform the police. But other than that, I would do nothing more on this case. I would submit a report. But I'd probably never learn why the paintings were being damaged. It would be an unsolved case.

A failure.

Dave's face scrunched into a frown. "What is that banging noise?"

Until he mentioned it, I hadn't even noticed the dull thud that sounded from somewhere out in the office. "I think it's Rodney working on the new scanners." I sighed as I looked around. "Why do we have new scanners?"

"He wants to put all the files on the computer to save space."

"So where will everything be stored?"

"On a computer."

"Whose computer?"

"I don't know. I'll let you guys figure that out."

"You're not going to like it if we store all the invoice records on your computer, then have to come in here anytime we needed to look something up."

"Got that right."

"But I'm not going to like it if you store all the client files on my computer. Then if I'm doing payroll, I'd have to stop anytime you need to look up an address or Brittany needed to reference a report."

"Okay, so don't use ours."

"I'm just trying to get you to see that this is a complicated issue. If we're going to go paperless, we need a computer network and a good tech person."

"Whatever."

"Rodney is not a good tech person. He has hired two temps to scan documents, most of which are already in electronic format."

Dave winced.

I decided to let it all out now. He might pull the "I'm

the boss" speech again, but I was at least going to have my say first. "Rodney bought two new scanners when at least one of the printers we already have has a scan function. In the time he's been here, he's destroyed the place, cost a small fortune, and taken the coffeepot hostage. And yet you still refuse to fire him. What gives? Is he the brother of some girl you're trying to impress?"

"No. But close."

"Huh?"

"His uncle is CEO of Consolidated Building. When I went to discuss what our firm could do for his business, he in turn suggested what his nephew might be able to offer our firm. It seemed like a win-win at the time."

"And now?"

He sighed and rubbed his face. "Well, with the added business, we've still taken in more than he's cost us in incense."

"And printers. And temps. And electricians."

"Yeah," he said as he waved expansively, "all of them, too."

"But you haven't even signed the contract with them yet." I pointed to the envelope on his desk that I had been nagging him about for at least two weeks.

"It'll get done. Don't worry."

"So he stays?"

"For now, yeah."

"We can't work like this, Dave."

He smiled. "You'll find a way to make it work. I'm sure you will."

Oh yeah? Well I'm not. But I didn't say it aloud. I just hoped he could read it in my expression before I turned to stalk out the door.

This was just great. Since I wasn't on assignment at the Blue Moon anymore, I would be stuck in the office full-time with my oblivious brother, the office maximizing money waster, and the clueless intern.

Actually, that wasn't fair. Right now, Brittany was coming out miles ahead of either Dave or Rodney in the intelligence department. But that still didn't mean I looked forward to working closely with her again.

And the whole thing was so frustrating. If I just had some proof that Vicki was behind the vandalism at the Blue Moon, everything would be different. Or if I had just managed to convince Vicki to confess.

If only I were better at reading people, the way Dave was.

The door intercom beeped.

"Can you see who that is?" I called to Brittany, who was sitting closer to the front window than I was. We weren't expecting anyone, and the UPS guy had already come and gone. The last thing I wanted to deal with at the moment was some crazy person from off the street or the subject of an investigation who had recognized Dave's car and come up to confront us.

Rodney hit the buzzer to unlock the downstairs door. "This is a professional place of business and we should be accessible to the public during business hours."

I turned to him, my annoyance now matched by alarm. "I've told you before, it's not safe to let people in without knowing who they are and why they're here."

"It was a really big guy, too," Brittany said, eyes wide as saucers. "I hope he's not mad at us about something."

We all listened to the sound of heavy footsteps on the

stairs and stared uneasily as our large visitor knocked on the door, vibrating the wood with each hammering blow.

"Uh, would one of you girls get that, please?" Rodney waved toward the door. "Greet our guest in a professional manner."

I reached for the heavy-duty stapler, which I figured I could use like a club if I had to. If this guy was belligerent, I hoped he'd take his rage out on Rodney first. Stepping forward, I pulled the door open, keeping myself hidden behind it and leaving Rodney in clear view.

"Does Karen Maxwell work here?"

At the sound of Brian's voice, I peered around the door sheepishly.

He smiled. "Oh, there you are."

"How did you know where I worked?"

"You told me."

"Oh."

"I take it you know this gentleman?" Rodney asked.

"Uh, yes. Brian, I'd like you to meet Rodney Cadle, Brittany Rosencrans, and. . ." I was drawing a blank on the names of the two temps.

"Andrea and Julie," Brittany prompted.

I smiled at her gratefully. "Thank you. Guys, this is Brian Kieffer."

Everybody exchanged generic greetings and then stood awkwardly as if we were all uncertain what to do with ourselves. I kept wondering why Brian was there. And I think we all felt embarrassed at having been scared by his pounding on the door.

"Why don't I show you around the office?" I suggested to Brian to end the uncomfortable moment.

"Sure. Great." He smiled and suddenly I felt kind of melty inside and didn't really care why he was there anymore.

The others went back to work. "Is that your boyfriend?" Brittany whispered as she passed me.

I nodded.

"He's *phat*."

"He's. . ." then I remembered what Vicki had explained. "Thanks," I whispered back with a smile.

Brian was facing the kitchen, so I steered him there. "This is the kitchen," I pointed out.

He pointed toward the computer on the counter. "But why is there a—"

"Don't ask. And that"—I steered him toward the back of the office and nodded toward the bathroom—"should be obvious."

He nodded.

"Over here we have. . ." I stopped because I couldn't remember what Rodney had moved over into the area where we used to have the copier and fax machine. So I continued on to my private office space in the closet. "Anyway, my desk is over here."

"This looks cozy."

It probably would be, if he were in it with me. I suppressed the urge to drag him inside to find out. "And this—" I tripped over a stack of files. "This is a mess. I don't know what any of this is at the moment!" I said a little crossly, letting my anger get the better of me again. I was embarrassed, both at my awkwardness and the fact that the place was such a mess.

Brian took my arm. "It's okay."

"I'll introduce you to my brother." I nodded toward Dave's office. "The boss."

"I met him, remember? At the House."

He was referring to the 1776 House, where Dave had met Brian during my investigation, in which Brian was one of the suspects. "You should meet him again," I suggested. "He'll look at you very differently now."

I knocked on Dave's door.

"Come in."

My hand tingled a little as I turned the doorknob. With my parents living in Arizona and so far removed from my daily life, introducing Brian to my brother suddenly seemed a really big deal. "Dave, this is Brian. I think you met at the 1776 House?"

His chair lurched forward as he stood to shake hands. "Oh, the blacksmith, right."

"Ah, today I'm just an ordinary office guy."

"Where do you work?"

"URS. In Hunt Valley."

"Hey, that's a drive, isn't it?" Dave leaned back against his credenza. "What brings you here?"

"Your sister."

I could feel my face heat up like a toaster oven.

"Karen?" Dave blinked in surprise. Then he looked from Brian to me a few times. Then he just looked at me. "I need to talk to you later."

"It's okay." For some odd reason, seeing Dave look nervous suddenly made me relax. He was either worried that my attraction to a suspect had marred my judgment in the last case or he was worried that his sister was dating an ax murderer.

"We'll let you get back to work." I started to push Brian toward the door.

"Good seeing you again." Brian nodded toward Dave.

I pulled the door shut behind us quickly and let out a little giggle. "Did you see the look he gave you? And then the look he gave me?"

"He's just being a good brother."

"I'm not sure if he was being the boss or the brother at that moment. Maybe both." As I spoke I gradually realized that Brittany, Rodney, and both temps were watching us.

"So can you break for lunch?" Brian asked. "I wanted to take you out."

I heard murmurings from the girls about how sweet that was, or cute, or something. All I knew was that even if I hadn't had time, I would have taken it anyway just to get away from the audience. "Let me get my purse."

⚊

"So why did you come down here?" I asked after we'd stepped out into the sun and started to stroll toward the center of town.

"I told you. To take you to lunch."

"But we hadn't planned a date."

"I know. You said I needed to be more spontaneous."

I stopped. "And so you did it? Just like that?"

"Well, I did ask my boss if it was okay for me to take a long lunch today."

I looked up at him, as wind whipped tendrils of dark hair around his face, lit with that smile. . . "Thank you," I said finally.

"No, thank you," he insisted, taking my hand in his as we turned the corner onto Main Street. "You reminded me of an important part of my life that's missing. 'Consider the ravens: they neither sow nor reap, they have neither storehouse nor barn, and yet God feeds them.'"

What the. . ."You're missing the ravens?" I asked. "You mean like the football team?"

He laughed. "No. What I meant with that quote is that the ravens don't plan ahead. They're not always working toward the future. Yet God takes care of them."

He looked to the side, where the creek that runs beneath the buildings on that side of Main Street is visible for a short stretch. Together we walked toward the sound of rushing water.

"Sometimes," he continued, "I just need to live in the moment like the ravens. Enjoy what's happening now, thank God for each minute of life he's given me and make the most of it."

He did it again, brought God into the middle of a date. It just didn't seem right somehow. God belonged in church, not out in the sun and wind, holding hands with a boyfriend.

I couldn't enjoy the moment if God was there.

Could I?

As kind of a test, I gave Brian's hand a squeeze and he pulled me closer, as both of us stopped to gaze down at the water as it rushed below us.

Neither of us spoke for a long while. "I forget most of the time," I said finally, "that there's a creek running through here. It's odd, isn't it? That I could be so oblivious to something that keeps rushing on and on like that?"

"I think it's human nature. We get wrapped up in ourselves and don't notice the rest of life going on around us. And God is watching over it all, waiting to help."

"Waiting to help? I thought God was pretty much watching to see if we did what we were supposed to." I waved toward a rustic wooden reindeer with a light-up nose. "You know, like Santa."

"God's always ready to help, but He waits for us to ask."

I was going to ask if He'd help by going away if I asked, but I decided not to. Brian might find that offensive. He seemed pretty comfortable with the idea of God being around all the time.

The talk of God made me think of church. "Your play is this weekend, isn't it?"

He stared into the dark water. "Yep."

"You don't seem very happy about it."

His face brightened as he turned to me. "Oh, it'll be great. I wish some of the kids had made it to more practices, but I have to remember that they're busy, and even if they don't know things as well as I'd like, they each have something valuable to contribute. So in the end, it'll be a great show."

I stole a glance at him. "Do you ever get tempted to kick them out? When they miss too many practices?"

"Yeah, I guess I do. But then I remember that if God gave up on me every time I didn't do something I was supposed to, I'd be in trouble. So if He can keep the faith in me, I guess I can keep the faith in others."

"Is that why you always say 'keep the faith'?"

"I always say that?"

"On the phone you do. On messages and stuff."

"I didn't realize. . .but I guess so."

Could he really be as forgiving as all that? Working with some of those kids would drive me crazy. "You don't even wish you could lose the kid who keeps hitting people with all the props from old plays?"

"Ben? Nah. He's about the only one who's made it to all the rehearsals. He'll probably end up feeding everyone else their lines."

"What about the Disgruntled Doll? Has she come to any practices?"

"Only two. She's had basketball every other day. But she has a good strong voice and she can hit the harmony notes the others can't seem to find. The musical numbers don't quite work without her."

Well the musical numbers certainly did sound terrible, but I wasn't sure the presence of any one person would make them that much better.

He cleared his throat. "I know I've asked a lot from you these last few weeks, and I hope you'll forgive me for asking again, but I could really use your help with the dress rehearsal Friday night if you can make it."

I squeezed his hand. "Hey, I've come this far. It's just one more."

"Great, thank you."

Especially if it rains, I found myself thinking, remembering the last time we'd kissed. Maybe it was the sound of water again now, as the creek rushed from the bridge to the culvert ahead.

And maybe he was thinking of the same thing, because he snuggled close against my side. "I like this."

"Me, too." I turned to look at him. "Wait, what is it that you like?"

"Being close. You, talking to me without apologizing."

"Apologizing?"

"You're always getting upset, apologizing, and then you just stop talking. And that's sort of it."

"It is?" I winced. "I mean, I didn't realize it was that bad."

"It isn't today. Maybe I should interrupt you at the office more often. It might only work when you're having a good day on the job, though."

"I'm having a pretty crummy day, actually. I just got fired from my second case."

And I told him all about it, about my frustration with being so close to making the case, my frustration at not figuring out how to get Vicki to confess, my fears about losing this part of my job. I dumped all of this on Brian while we ate burgers at the Phoenix Emporium. And I didn't worry about boring him or making him tired of me. I didn't even think of it until later and by then I didn't care. It just felt so good to let it all out.

"Thank you for sharing," Brian said as he walked me back to the office.

"What? You don't have enough problems in your life so you needed to share some of mine?"

"I wanted to. I've unloaded so much on you about Chloe, and I guess I was afraid I scared you off or something."

"Hardly." I smiled. "In fact, I believe you owe me. Next time I want more from you, more guilt, more worries, something."

"Fair enough." He leaned in to give me a kiss on the cheek. "See you on Friday," he said in a low voice, staying close a little longer than I'd expected.

I kind of wished I could follow him back to his office

instead of going back upstairs to my own.

When I got back, Brittany informed me that Rodney and Dave were at lunch.

"And the temps?"

"Dave told them to take a nice long lunch break, too."

"That was unusually generous."

"Not really. We don't pay them for the time they're at lunch."

Once again, Brittany surprised me with an observation. Maybe she wasn't as dim-witted as I'd assumed. She didn't take to clerical work well, but that was probably because she wasn't interested in clerical work. She observed details and she could recall them. That was an important skill for an investigator. And though she had been hired as a typist and clerk, she no doubt applied for the job because she ultimately wanted to be an investigator, not a secretary.

What was it that Brian had said about the play? Everyone had something to contribute, right? Had I been refusing to let Brittany contribute to the firm?

I had been so worried that she might get the opportunity to do investigative work without putting in years of clerical work as I had done that I didn't even consider whether she might have more talent for it than I did. The firm would benefit from having its employees do the jobs they did best.

Rodney pointed that out on his first day.

And it took me this long to see the truth, because I was jealous.

Jealous and so very often annoyed. Brittany had apparently taken a phone message for me while I was out at lunch and, as usual, it was mostly illegible. "Brittany, what is this supposed to mean?" I tried to read the scrawl aloud. 'Onam called about the. . .something zoo'?"

She slipped on the clogs she had kicked off under her desk and shuffled over to me. "Doreen called about the Blue Moon."

"The insurance claim. Thank you!" Rather than try to read the number on the message itself, I looked up Doreen in my rolodex.

"The claim was withdrawn," she informed me when her receptionist put the call through.

"What?" I hadn't even been able to find a working pen to take notes.

"It was filed by someone named Geraldine Miller. But it was shortly withdrawn. That's why I had so much trouble finding information about it."

I scribbled down the word "withdrawn."

"So okay," I asked, "what does that mean?"

"It can mean any number of things. But usually it means the client offered to settle out of pocket before a record was created."

I thought about that for a moment. "Geraldine Miller was the artist of one of the damaged paintings, and hers was on consignment. Did this mean that she filed a claim and the owners of the store offered to pay for the damage themselves?"

"Very likely. But I can't tell. Why don't you ask them?"

I decided not to admit that they'd fired me. "Well, hey, Doreen thanks a billion. I owe you."

"It was nothing."

"It sure wasn't. It makes a huge difference."

"I know. I was just saying that. I'm sure I'll have a favor

for you guys by the end of the week."

I laughed, and she quickly joined in. Both of us knew that was true enough. Doreen hated her firm's investigators and was always looking for an excuse to get us to check out something for her.

After I hung up the phone, I spun around in my chair, in a very Dave-like motion. So Mr. and Mrs. P. had likely compensated Geraldine Miller for damage to a painting they held in low regard. And they had not filed a claim for damage to the Tollefsen paintings they owned. That made them look like unlikely suspects.

And it made Vicki look all the more guilty. She was taking advantage of two employers who had always treated her well, from what I could see.

It wasn't right.

And I hadn't been able to do much to get it to stop. I couldn't bring Dave in now. He didn't even want me working on the case anymore. What else could I do?

I spun around in my chair again. And ended up facing Brittany.

She was young and she looked very vulnerable, although I was pretty sure it was mostly an act. But it was a very convincing act. If she could convince Vicki that she was just a vulnerable, hurt kid, it might bring out Vicki's protective instinct. Since Vicki wanted to protect innocent frogs from vicious chefs at Tersiguel's, she might also feel the need to help protect college girls from boyfriends who wanted to break up with them.

I walked over to Brittany's desk. The image of computer solitaire quickly disappeared from her computer screen.

"How old are you, Brittany?"

"Twenty-one. Well, I'll be twenty-two next month."

Old enough. Besides, I would send her in when the business was open, with other employees around. It wouldn't be dangerous. Mr. and Mrs. P. didn't know Brittany worked for us, so if the conversation went badly, it wouldn't reflect on the firm.

"I was, uh, wondering if you could help me with my investigative assignment." Once I choked out the first few words, the rest came easy.

"You've got a new assignment?"

"Er, no."

"But you were fired from the Blue Moon."

It shouldn't have surprised me that she knew, but it did.

"Uh, yeah, I was. But I still have to send the client the report. And I'm missing a few details. So I was wondering if you could help fill them in."

"Cool." Her eyes grew wide as they had earlier, not with fear this time but with excitement.

"Okay, I need you to go down to the Blue Moon and pretend like your boyfriend just broke up with you. Maybe you could be talking to him on your cell phone while you're in the store. But I need to make sure that a certain employee there sees you very upset. Do you think you can do that?"

"No problem. You can call me, so the phone rings while I'm there."

"Good idea. Now the employee is Vicki Bourbonnais, and she's just a little older than you, blond hair, petite, moves and talks like a flight attendant."

"Are there other employees who look like her or will it be obvious?"

Again I was surprised by her thoughtful approach. "It should be obvious. I want you to get her sympathy and see if you can get her to talk about her boyfriend. See if she gives you any ideas for hanging onto reluctant boyfriends."

"Not because you think I need a boyfriend, right?"

I took a deep breath. If I was going to ask her to do this, I had to tell her why and hope that she wouldn't spill information to the wrong person. "No. It's because I think Vicki is damaging paintings to get revenge on a painter who stole her boyfriend's idea. I think she was somehow expecting her boyfriend to be grateful for this, grateful enough to take her back."

She just looked at me.

"Sounds crazy, I know."

"Yeah," she said slowly. "But I guess I've heard worse."

"You have? What. . .never mind. You know what I'm after, right?"

"You want me to encourage her to tell me all about how she's getting her boyfriend back."

"Right."

"When do you want me to go?"

I glanced at my watch. Two-thirty. Vicki would be there until five. "Anytime."

She reached into a drawer and grabbed a bag that was either a very small backpack or a purse with too many straps. "Call me in an hour."

"It won't take you that long to walk down there."

"I have to shop elsewhere for a while so I don't look suspicious."

I think I must have narrowed my eyes at her as if to

suggest I thought she was taking advantage of the situation.

"What? I haven't had my lunch break yet. Or not all of it, anyway."

I waved her on. "Go. I'll call you at 3:30."

When the door closed behind her the office seemed very quiet. And the clock moved very slowly.

At 3:30 I called; she answered on the second ring.

"Oh, Drake, it's you," she gushed.

Drake? She expected Vicki to believe she had a boy-friend named Drake? What was this, a romance novel?

"Hey Brittany," I said, lowering my voice just for fun. "I want to break up with you."

"But why?" she exclaimed dramatically.

"You have the wrong color hair," I explained, in an even lower voice.

"But I can change. Give me a chance!"

"I don't like your shoes."

"You don't understand. None of this matters. We belong together."

"Gotta run," I said in my lowest voice yet. "Wrestling shark football is on. Dave's coming out of his office so I'm going to go now."

I wasn't sure Dave would approve of this, sending Brittany in on a case where we'd already been fired and wouldn't make any more money. I decided we wouldn't tell him about it unless it worked. If it didn't, I would tell him that Brittany left early to do me a favor, which was completely true.

She wouldn't be back until after I'd left to go home.

I wished I was a painting on the wall at the Blue Moon so I could see what was happening.

Evan wouldn't talk to me when he came home after school.

"How was your day?"

He shrugged.

"I'll bet everyone's getting anxious to be out of school for Christmas break."

No response.

"Did you remember to turn in your research report for the science fair?"

Still no response.

"Evan, answer me!"

"Why?" he snapped. "You won't believe me anyway."

"Yes, I. . ." The words trailed off as I gave up. He wouldn't listen to me no matter what I said.

When the phone rang a few minutes later, I hoped it was Brian.

It was Brittany.

"Hi, um, Karen? I wanted to tell you what happened in the Blue Moon."

I couldn't tell from the tone of her voice whether she'd had any luck or not. "Are you at the office?"

"No. That was one thing I was going to ask you. I don't have to go back, do I? Because by the time I get there it will just be time to go home anyway."

"Yeah, no, don't worry about going back. So where are you?" I hoped she was far enough from the Blue Moon that she could talk without being overheard by someone involved.

"I'm at Caplans. Well, and at Yates Grocery."

For a moment I was confused about how she could

be in two places at once. "You're walking down the street, aren't you?"

"Well, yeah." She made it sound as if I would be a complete idiot for thinking anything else.

"Okay, so what happened?"

"Vicki was behind the counter and when you called, I sort of walked over closer and then I sat down like I was all in shock about something. I sat on something that looked expensive so I could get her attention."

"Good."

"And so I was crying and she offered me a tissue and then just like you said, she started talking about how boys don't know when they've found the right girl and I can get him back if I just try."

"Did she talk about getting her boyfriend back?"

"Sort of. She said I needed to have a plan like she did, and work each day to make something happen."

Each day. Did that mean she had been damaging more things that I wasn't aware of? Or was she just leaving little cryptic signs like frog stickers on Craig's mailbox? "She didn't tell you what her plan was?"

"When I asked, she said it was a trade secret."

We were the tiniest step closer, but still a long leap away from proof.

"She did say, though, that I would have to be willing to take risks."

"Did she say what kind of risks?"

"Well, she said I couldn't worry about being embarrassed because in the end it would be worth it. And I shouldn't worry about making people mad."

"Sounds like you talked to her for quite awhile."

"Yeah. I just left, in fact. She gave me the rest of the tissues, which is good because we're out at the apartment."

"Good job. I think tomorrow we should go shopping."

"Really?"

"To the Blue Moon. You can tell me all about your date with a great guy you just met. Craig Freels."

"Is that her boyfriend?"

"Yep."

"Ooh, Karen, I didn't think you could be so cruel."

"Oh yeah, I'm a mom, remember? We all have a cruel streak. Besides, this girl has caused thousands of dollars' worth of damage. She needs to be stopped, and nice isn't getting it done."

"Yeah, I guess so. Well, I'll see you tomorrow then."

She clicked off without saying good-bye, which is probably old-fashioned now.

So Brittany the worthless college intern had succeeded where I had failed. How did that feel?

She hadn't completely succeeded, of course, but she made a lot more progress than I had, getting Vicki to talk about Craig. I would have to show the girl more respect in the future, even if she had the penmanship of a limp-wristed squid.

17

Brittany grabbed my arm just before we walked into the Blue Moon the next morning. "Aren't you scared?"

"No," I lied. "What would I be scared of?"

"They fired you. I'd be afraid to go back in if I were you. They'll probably say something really embarrassing or insulting. Or they might call the police and have you thrown out."

"I'm not worried," I lied again. "You can't think about embarrassment, not on this job." I pulled her aside and lowered my voice because this reminded me of something important that we hadn't discussed. "What we should be worried about is the possibility of Vicki turning violent if she thinks you're dating her boyfriend. We want to upset her so she will lose her composure and say something she wouldn't otherwise. But we don't want her to come after you with a knife. So when we bring up the subject—"

"A knife!" Brittany shuddered but tried to laugh it off. "Does she carry weapons to work?"

"I don't know, but if nothing else, she can grab the pair of scissors they keep under the counter. We don't want her to come after you with *anything*. So when we start the conversation, I want us to be near the door, with me in between you and Vicki. If she gets scary on us, run for the door and don't look back, understand?"

"Um, yeah."

"I mean it. Don't look back like people always do in the movies."

"Yeah, then they trip on something and have to crawl forward while the monster gets closer and closer and—"

"Well, hopefully it won't come to that. But I just wanted to make sure we have an exit plan in place." Of course the exit plan was always "run" for me, but I needed to make sure that she was aware of it.

"What if she comes after *you* with the knife?"

"I'll race you to the door. But she won't bother me."

"Why not?"

I tried to smile, but it probably came out as more of a wistful grimace. "I'm not a threat. Craig isn't going to consider dating an old woman like me."

"You're not old. Not that old, anyway."

"Thanks. I think. Let's go." I held open the door and held my breath at the same time.

"Hi, Karen." Vicki looked up in surprise when the bell on the door jingled. "I didn't expect to see you here today."

"Yeah, well, I needed to return my key." I had rehearsed my reason yesterday. There were a few problems with the plan, though. For starters, I was going to have to lie like a rug and that made me very uneasy.

Her eyes widened in surprise. "I didn't know you had a key. You always waited for me to let you in."

That was one of the problems. "I forgot they gave me one."

"I can take it back for you." She held out her hand.

That was another one. I couldn't give her a key since I'd never had one to begin with. "That's okay, I'll take it back myself and say hi to Mr. and Mrs. P. while I'm there."

Problem three. I couldn't let them see me.

And now to explain Brittany's presence. . . "I think you met my niece yesterday?"

"Yes. I hope things are going better today?" Vicki's eyes were full of genuine sympathy.

Brittany nodded enthusiastically. "Much."

"I sent her in yesterday to return the key, but then she got a phone call and I guess she forgot."

"Yeah," Brittany said sheepishly. "I got a little carried away."

And here was the perfect opening for them to pick up where they left off yesterday. "I'm going to run back with this key," I said to Brittany, waving toward the pocket in my jacket that contained a nickel, a half-used tissue, and no key. "If you just want to shop or whatever for a minute."

"Sure."

I hurried back toward the office, hoping she would keep Vicki engaged but not say anything important until I returned. As I got closer, I could hear Mr. and Mrs. P. conversing in the office over the sound of rustling newspaper. There was no way I could walk in there. My steps got slower and slower as I kept checking back to see if Vicki was watching.

Brittany suddenly pointed to something on the front wall, causing Vicki to turn around. Thank you, Brittany! As soon as Vicki's back was turned, I ducked behind an armoire. I had an imaginary conversation with Mr. and Mrs. P. *How are you? I'm fine. Sorry I forgot to return this key. Well, good seeing you again.* When I peeked around the edge of the armoire, Vicki was facing me, so I would have to wait until she turned away again to stage my "return" from the office.

I figured Brittany would distract her again as she'd done before. But as the seconds ticked by, it didn't happen.

Minutes went by with the two of them talking and me just stuck in the back hoping that Mr. and Mrs. P. wouldn't decide to come out into the store anytime soon.

Come on, Brittany. I tried to send a telepathic message. *Make Vicki turn around again.*

My telepathic message of course had no effect.

But I *could* send her a telephone message. If I knew how to send a text message, this would be a great time to use that knowledge. But I'd never had any interest in typing messages with my thumbs, so that was out. I dialed Brittany's number. I wouldn't be able to talk, because then they'd both hear me, but maybe at the sight of my number, Brittany would realize that she needed to distract Vicki again.

"Do you need to get that?" Vicki asked as the phone rang.

Brittany flipped it open. "No. It's just him again."

"But this is a good sign," Vicki insisted excitedly. "You should answer. Let him know you're available."

"But I'm not." Brittany flipped the phone closed. "I've found someone else."

Wait! I screamed silently. *Wait for me to get up there! Wait until you're near the door!* I inched closer to the edge of the armoire, ready to run out if she kept going.

"Hey, can you tell me what the symbol on the front of that thing means?" Brittany pointed to a cabinet in the front of the store.

Yes! Brittany was moving toward the door.

"Symbol?" Vicki asked.

"Yeah, look." Brittany walked toward the door, beckoning for Vicki to follow. "This flowery thing here."

When Vicki moved, I sort of hopped into place, where

I would be if I had come out of the office instead of behind the armoire. And I headed toward the front of the store.

Vicki was bending down examining a picture of a flower when I caught up with them.

"I think that's a flower," she said.

"I've, uh, heard that people put symbols on things t—to make it their territory." Brittany's voice began to falter as if she couldn't quite figure out what to say. "You know, like gang markings."

Vicki looked at her as if she'd turned purple. "On antique furniture?"

"Maybe it's like a Masonic symbol," I suggested.

"No, I think it's just a flower for decoration." Vicki stood, dusted off her hands, and started back toward the counter.

Now she thought both of us were a little weird and she was getting away.

I hurried after her. "Vicki?" I stopped so she would have to stop to keep from looking rude.

"Yes?"

"I just wanted to thank you for helping my niece out when she was so upset yesterday."

"Hey, no problem."

"I felt bad that I wasn't there for her, and so it was great when she told me about all the strategies you gave her for dealing with stuff."

"I'm glad I could help."

"And now I've met the greatest guy," Brittany added, on cue.

"Tell us about him," I said, making eye contact with Vicki as if to say, *look how you helped her*.

"He's really cute, of course," Brittany started dreamily, "but he doesn't act like he knows it. He's really sweet, and a little shy. I think he's some kind of artist."

At the word "artist," Vicki's eyes brightened. She was showing more than polite interest now.

"Oh," I said. "Where did you meet him?"

"Down by the river. He was walking his pet ferret. I think he called her Gypsy. Isn't that cute?"

Vicki's hands clenched into fists at her sides.

"We talked for hours. It's like we've known each other forever. He told me he thought I was amazing, that he'd never felt this way about a girl before." Brittany blinked, her eyes starry with happiness. I could almost picture this nonexistent encounter. "He even asked if he could kiss me. And I said, 'Craig, no one asks if they can kiss someone, it just hap—"

"No," Vicki insisted in an unsteady voice. "No, it doesn't happen that way."

"What's wrong?" Brittany asked with an innocent smile. She was probably overdoing it a bit on the innocence, but other than that, she was perfect.

Vicki seemed to be in shock. She kept her gaze focused on a chair in front of her and spoke as if she were the only one in the room. "He's supposed to talk to me, not to some silly college girl. I can't believe he would do this to me."

"Do you know this guy?" I asked.

"He's a really good kisser," Brittany said, with a mischievous glance at me.

That got Vicki's full attention. Her gaze immediately shifted from the chair to Brittany, her look of distant sadness replaced by cold fury. I realized then that I had not kept myself between the two girls as I'd planned to. Before I could do anything to protect Brittany, Vicki reached out and slapped her across the face.

"You weren't supposed to kiss him!" She hissed. "You were supposed to kiss your own boyfriend, not mine."

"Well, excuse me for being prettier." Brittany smirked as she took a step back. "I didn't know he was your boyfriend, anyway."

The fact that Brittany was goading Vicki on made it more likely that Vicki would completely lose her cool and spill her guts. It also made it more likely that she would spill Brittany's guts instead. "I think maybe you should go now," I said softly to Brittany.

"You've ruined everything!" Vicki advanced slowly toward her nemesis.

"Go." I nudged Brittany toward the door. "Please."

Brittany ignored me and flipped her hair back over her shoulder like a cover model as she smirked again at Vicki. "You must be the loser girlfriend he told me about. He said he'd never date someone like you again in like a gazillion years."

I winced. Maybe we had to be this mean to get results, but I didn't like it and would have tried another tactic first. And it could be dangerous, because while so far Vicki kept her mounting rage in check, she might suddenly try to—

Without warning, Vicki lunged forward, clawing at Brittany's eyes. I pushed Brittany back into the glass of the door. "Get out of here! Now!"

Then I grabbed Vicki to pull her the opposite direction. "Let her go, she's not worth it."

"She stole my boyfriend!"

"I'm sorry to say this, Vicki," I said, steadily lowering my voice to calm her down, "but it sounds like Craig doesn't see himself as your boyfriend anymore."

She jerked away from me, but Brittany was long gone, and Vicki made no move to chase after her. "Of course he does," Vicki insisted. "He is. He just doesn't realize it yet."

"What are you going to do to make him realize it?" I asked softly. "Are you going to do something to show him that you belong together?"

She sighed. "I have. I've done so much and he just doesn't get it. He doesn't understand how love works."

"How does it work?"

"He needs me. I can do so much for him."

"What have you done?"

"Shows." She waved toward the paintings on the walls. "In the best galleries."

"He didn't want shows."

"He does." She tucked her hair behind her ear. "He doesn't realize it yet."

"What about revenge against the man who stole from him? Did he realize he needed revenge against Tollefsen?"

"Yes!" She turned to stare directly into my eyes, and it took all my willpower not to step back in fear. For a few seconds, I was staring into the eyes of a wild animal.

"He didn't understand," she continued. "But he will. And then he will be so grateful. He will beg me to take him back."

"What did he need to do to get revenge?"

"Tollefsen stole his idea, his genius. He stole his will to create. He destroyed all the works Craig might have created. So he needed to strike back. To destroy something of Tollefsen's."

"To destroy artwork of Tollefsen's?"

"Yes."

"But would he do it?"

"No. He wasn't ready. He needed someone strong to help him. He needed me."

I took a deep breath. "Did you destroy some of Tollefsen's paintings to help Craig?"

"I had to. Don't you see?"

I shook my head. "You didn't hurt Tollefsen. You hurt the people who owned the paintings you destroyed. Mr. and Mrs. Photopoulos."

She looked at me blankly. "No, I didn't. I set it up to look as if vandals from outside caused the damage. You know, other paintings, antiques—stuff all over the store. So the insurance company will cover the expense."

"They won't report it to the insurance company."

She waved a hand dismissively. "That's their problem. I made it easy for them. They don't know what they're doing in this business."

"It's your problem, too. What you did, what you just admitted to doing, is illegal."

"Hmph," she sniffed. "Damages can all be settled with a check."

"A check," I repeated blankly.

"My dad can take care of it. Money can buy more paintings, if that's what we need here."

"You have that kind of money?"

Vicki put on a condescending smile. "My parents own paintings worth more than any of those silly Tollefsens. Galleries full of them."

"Then why are you working here, instead of for them?"

"They wanted me to gain experience in different settings, to see how different firms operate. And we don't want to operate anything like this. I can't wait until they tell me I've been here long enough so I can leave."

So the happy employee behavior had all been an act. She was just serving an internship, waiting for her parents to decide she was ready to trade up. This explained why Vicki was always trying to move things around and acting as if she owned the gallery. She was probably pretending she did.

"If you tell Mr. and Mrs. P. about your plan to help Craig," I said dryly, "I'm sure they will be happy to tell your parents that you've been here long enough."

"Of course," she said, as if that were a good idea. "Let's go tell them right now." She started back toward the office.

This girl was crazy. Though it made my job ten times easier if she confessed directly to the clients like this, I still felt a need to warn her, because I don't think she really understood the implications of what she'd done.

"Wait, Vicki, you do realize that you can go to jail for this?"

She laughed. "Not a chance. We have more than enough paintings to convince Mr. and Mrs. P. to drop any charges."

This may very well have been true, but it was not comforting to think that rich crazy people were probably buying themselves out of trouble—and of help—all the time.

So when she made her frank, matter-of-fact confession to a stunned Mr. and Mrs. P., I quietly recommended they call the police and have her arrested. That might get her parents and maybe even Vicki herself to realize that she needed help.

They were too stunned to react to much of anything I said. They plainly had thought quite highly of Vicki, and her betrayal and new attitude of disinterested contempt seemed to wound them deeply. After awhile, Mrs. P. shifted some of her energy from shock and hurt to anger. And then she called 911.

After much debating with my conscience, I told Mr. and Mrs. P. about Eric's involvement in the vandalism. They were devastated but decided that since they'd known him so long, they would confront him themselves the next time he was in the store rather than have him arrested. Vicki had told them that she asked Eric to "help" her with the antiques, and they knew he would probably do anything for her. They didn't really think he was at fault.

All the time we waited for the police and discussed Eric's participation in the crime, Vicki fussed with her hair and fixed her makeup. She left calmly, saying only what was necessary in response to the officer's questions. And she walked out with him as if he were carrying her bags on a shopping trip rather than arresting her on vandalism charges. She held her head high and seemed to pay no attention to the officer or to any of the rest of us.

And then she was gone.

And it was all over.

18

At the sound of Dave's heavy footsteps on the stairs, I decided to cut short my phone conversation with Brian. "I'll see you at the dress rehearsal tonight."

"Right. Congrats again on the case."

I knew what was coming next. "Keep the faith!" I said quickly, just as he did.

He laughed. "I guess you're right about that, too. Man, I am so predictable."

"Not always." I smiled at the phone receiver, even though he couldn't see. "'Bye."

"'Bye."

As I hung up the phone, I studiously ignored the untenable mess surrounding me. I had to. The office that used to be shabby but neat was now tornado chic. We might have designer counters in our kitchen, but we couldn't use the room to make coffee or reheat lunch leftovers. We had plants and fountains and designer lighting fixtures, but they only illuminated piles of disorganized file folders. And Dave had barreled into several stacks, so they had turned to paper mudslides, sweeping along bits of old wrappers, sticky notes, and paper clips in their path of destruction. I said I couldn't work like this and I was right. It took all my energy to ignore my surroundings. Soon I would be sitting on my desk burning incense.

I watched the door as Dave's footsteps drew closer.

"Guess what?" I asked as soon as the door swung open.

"You made it to work before me?"

"As if that was even worth mentioning. No, I made the case at the Blue Moon."

His forehead wrinkled in confusion. "You told me that on Wednesday. You knew the culprit and were going to put it in your report."

"I got her to *confess*. In front of the clients."

"How? I thought they—"

"They even had her arrested."

"Wow, that's great, but if they fired us then I still don't—"

I held up my wrist. "Look at the time. I'd better get the weekly reports finished." I started back toward my desk. "Let me know if you make a coffee run."

"Karen, stop."

"Yes?" I asked innocently.

"How did you get a confession if you were off the case? Were you spending time that the firm couldn't bill? We lose money that way."

"Let me ask you something. Have you finished filling out the tears from this week?"

"No, but what does that—"

"How about last week?"

"No," he said, obviously annoyed at the interruption. "You know I don't always have time for all the paperwork."

"The firm can't bill for your hours without the tears. Eventually we estimate, but we have to way underestimate. We lose money that way, too."

He rubbed his chin. "I get it. But don't let it happen too often."

"You forget your tears every week."

"It's my firm. I'm allowed to cost us more often."

"Fair enough." I looked around. "Speaking of costing us money, where is Rodney?"

"He said he had to stop in at Consolidated Building this morning before he came in."

"He's milking this connection for all it's worth, isn't he?"

Dave paused for a moment, leaning back against a file cabinet. "He's not getting away with as much as you think."

"How so?"

"I had a little talk with his uncle yesterday. I said our administrative overhead was proving more costly than originally projected."

"So that. . ."

He grinned. "So that we would very likely have to raise our fees above the figure we originally discussed."

Excellent. I was worried Dave hadn't signed the contract from Consolidated Business. By holding off, he allowed himself space to renegotiate the fee. Once again, he proved that sometimes, he did know what he was doing.

"So." I smiled in return. "The uncle is going to have a little talk with the boy? Get him to tone things down a bit?"

Dave nodded. "Or give us more money to pay for it."

"More money won't necessarily erase the chaos."

"Creative chaos is a good thing. A neat desk is a sign of an inactive mind."

I pointed to his office. "And a messy desk can be a sign of an active rodent population. We have to find a balance here, somewhere. I need some order and predictability. You need space to do things your own way. And Rodney needs. . .well, I'm not sure. A lobotomy maybe."

"After he's talked with his uncle, he will be far more receptive to any suggestions you care to make. I guarantee it."

"Actually, it should be you making most of the suggestions. It's your office and you're the boss." I said it without the bitterness I felt earlier. It was true. It was his business, he built it with his former partner, and now that his partner had retired, the ultimate responsibility for its success or failure rested with him. He was entitled to be a little bossy at times. All that responsibility required a safety valve.

He looked at me strangely. "I never thought I'd hear you say that without sarcasm. You weren't being sarcastic, were you?"

"No. I wasn't. It's your firm and you know what you're doing far more often than I like to admit."

"Yeah, even slobs get things right sometimes, huh? But I have to admit, too, that all that annoying nagging about organization and paperwork is probably necessary. I asked Brittany to find an old client's address and it took her four hours to find the file."

This reminded me of something else I needed to admit, but I wasn't sure I was ready yet. Brittany deserved credit for helping to get the confession. It was a true team effort; neither of us could have done it alone. But I didn't feel like telling Dave that I'd asked her to go down to the Blue Moon after we'd been fired.

I cleared my throat. "She's been doing a good job lately."

"Are you saying that four hours is what we should be expecting for file retrieval?"

"No, the problem with the files is Rodney's reorganization. He keeps changing his system, so consequently we have no system at the moment."

"Maybe she can help him set up a new one."

"Maybe." She would hate that. I didn't much like the prospect either, but the thought of administrative work didn't send me into a catatonic state as it seemed to do to Brittany. "But I can help Rodney, since I know what's in the files better than anyone. And Brittany's time may be better put to use elsewhere. She's really been helping me out a lot lately."

Dave didn't ask at what, and I was glad. I wasn't quite ready to encourage him to give her more investigative work because that would potentially take work away from me. But if he proposed something and I thought she could do a better job at it, I would say so. "Well." I stood. "I want to get the report finished for the Blue Moon, but I'm going to need to head out for some coffee first. Can I bring you any?"

"Sure, I'll take—wait!" Dave looked at me with a gleam in his eyes before he turned to face the door. "I hear Rodney coming."

I heard the *clip-clop* of loafers but not quite as brisk as usual. I hoped his uncle hadn't been too hard on him.

When he opened the door, though, I could see that it was not chagrin that slowed his pace, but the large machine he was carrying in his arms.

"Is that what I think it is?"

Dave nodded. "An espresso machine. With a steam wand for making cappuccinos and lattes."

I looked from Dave to Rodney. "But I thought coffee wasn't as hip as tea?"

"Rodney makes an exception for lattes, apparently. His uncle told me about that one."

"Who paid for the machine?"

"I did." Dave smiled. "Happy birthday."

"My birthday's not until March."

"You know I won't remember your birthday on your actual birthday."

"Thank you." I gave him a rare hug. "I love lattes."

"I know. I also know you're too cheap to buy them most of the time."

"Yes! Thank you. You're a good boss, Boss."

He watched in satisfaction as Rodney carried the new machine into the kitchen. "I was trying to be a good brother this time."

"You're that, too." I grinned. "If there is such a thing."

"Stop it. I'll tell Mom!"

"That was always my line."

He sighed. "I know. I should have used it more often myself. Hey, you'd better get that."

"Get wha—" My words were interrupted by the ringing of the phone. "How did you know?"

He pointed to the phone on Brittany's desk. "The light always flashes once before it actually starts ringing."

"I never noticed."

"You're too busy with paperwork. I, on the other hand, keep my eyes open so that I can—"

I waved him off. "I'm going to answer the phone now." I picked up the receiver. "Good morning," I said, offering the generic greeting we always used for privacy.

"Hello," a rough voice said hesitantly. "Is this DS Investigations?"

"It is. How may I help you?"

The hoarse whisper was barely audible. "I want to talk to Karen Maxwell."

"This is Karen." I paused, not quite certain if I had the voice right. "Is this Mr. Photopoulos?"

"Yeah. Hey, I wanted to, uh, thank you again for following through after we, uh, you know. . ."

"You're welcome." It was quite a pleasure to be in a position to cut off his discomfort, instead of the other way around. "I should be sending out the final report later today," I assured him.

"I, uh, hope there's no hard feelings. You know my wife, she was getting a little fed up, and you know her temper. . ."

"It's okay. I understand." It might not have been okay if I hadn't been able to go back and finish the job, but I decided there was no point in thinking about that now. "It was a pleasure doing business with you."

"Yeah, um. . ." He sounded even more uncertain than at first. "I wanted your advice on something."

I smiled, even though he couldn't see. "Sure."

"Vicki's parents came in to talk to us. They offered to reimburse us for all the damage and your fees and everything if we drop the charges."

"Are you going to?"

"I don't know. That's what I wanted to ask you. Do you think we should?"

I pulled out Brittany's chair and sat down. "That's a tough one. I don't think she's a hardened criminal. I doubt she's likely to vandalize again and I hate to think of her in jail. But she went into this expecting her parents to buy her out of trouble. I think that has to end. She's got some problems and she needs some help. If you stand up to her parents and refuse their offer, they'll be forced to see that money can't solve everything."

"Yeah, I see what you're saying."

"But," I cautioned, "their offer to repay might be your best chance to be made whole monetarily out of this. If Vicki's in jail, she won't be able to pay you back anytime soon."

"Oh, yeah." He sounded as if he'd not thought of this before.

"So maybe you could accept, but make the deal contingent on psychiatric counseling or something."

"Oh, okay. Thanks for your help."

"Listen," I cautioned, "I'm not telling you what to do. I'm just giving you some things to think about."

"Right."

"You and Mrs. P. should talk about this and think about it carefully before you decide. Don't let them pressure you into making a decision too fast."

"Yeah, they've called twice this morning already. Well, thank you."

"You're welcome. I hope things work out."

"Yeah, me, too. Good-bye."

"Good-bye."

I hung up with a rare sense of satisfaction. For once, everything was reaching a nice state of closure. My second case was tied up and would be wrapped with a completed-report bow by the end of the day. Rodney and I would start to work on reorganizing the files and I would make sure that we located the file cabinets in places where they would not be likely to fall through the floor. Tonight was the last rehearsal for the play and soon that would be over, too. This weekend, I could finally relax.

19

I raised my glass of iced tea in a toast. "To a successful week."

"Hear, hear," Brian agreed.

Alicia clicked her glass against mine. "I guess my week wasn't as successful as Mom's. I haven't quite finished my project for world cultures. So I shouldn't be toasting yet."

"You're almost done, though." I turned to Evan. "And you won your soccer game yesterday, so that's two in a row for you."

He refused to pick up his glass or even look at me.

Brian smiled at Evan. "Karen didn't tell me you'd won. Congrats."

"Thanks," Evan mumbled, glancing at him for only a moment before returning his gaze to his plate.

"Are you feeling okay?" Brian asked him.

"Oh, he's fine," Alicia insisted as she reached for another piece of garlic bread. "He's just sulking because he's grounded. Get over it, dude," she advised as she turned toward her brother. "It's gonna happen a lot."

He sneered at her for a moment but said nothing. I was getting used to this and figured eventually he *would* get over it. It was a tough lesson but necessary. When he broke rules, like playing with the soccer ball in the house, he had to learn there were consequences. And when he lied about it, those consequences increased.

"Hey," I said, cheering myself with another good recollection. "I forgot to tell you that we made some progress with the mess in the office. Rodney agreed that we could put the files back in alphabetical order."

Brian grinned. "Do I want to know what order he planned to use instead?"

"I don't think he knew. He just had some ideas for classifying cases, and so we'll include the markings on the files, and maybe color coding, too. I think he's going to set up a system for finding similar cases when we need to cross-reference something. I don't need it because I remember most of the cases, but not everyone does, so this is actually a good idea. Do you want some more lasagna?"

"Sure. And speaking of good ideas, that was a good idea you had about cutting some of the dialogue in those two scenes, in the play." Brian held up his plate for another serving of pasta. "Jesse never could remember his lines and Casey only got to practice the scenes once, I think."

"I don't think they minded. And since the song they sang afterward had the same message, I don't think the audience missed anything." They should have been very grateful that I interceded on their behalf to remove some of the repetition. The play was still pretty juvenile, but at least it was shorter and some of the kids had fun hamming it up.

"I liked the play," Alicia said brightly. I was pretty certain she was lying, but whether she did it to make Brian feel good or because she was hoping to get a big role in a future production, I couldn't tell.

From the front bedroom upstairs, the dog started growling.

"Sounds like Tara disagrees with you," Brian joked.

The growl quickly escalated to a series of barks as the dog bounded down the stairs.

"Were we expecting anyone to come over?" I asked, since it looked like Tara was headed for the door.

"I don't think so," Alicia answered.

Tara first raced to the door then turned and headed toward the window that looked out over the side of the house.

"It's probably just the neighbor taking out the trash," I said reassuringly.

Sure enough, he appeared, dragging a trash can.

The dog was not reassured, however. She barked fiercely and suddenly jumped up, way up, bracing her front paws against the windows.

Her paws hit right where the top window overlapped with the bottom.

Right where the crystal cross had been hanging.

Oh no. I felt a hole in the pit of my stomach.

I had punished the wrong culprit. Evan hadn't broken the cross. Tara had. So that meant Evan hadn't lied about it, either. I had punished him wrongly.

"I am so sorry, Evan." I looked at him imploringly. "You told me the truth."

"About what?" Alicia asked. "What are you worried about?"

"I blamed Evan for breaking the crystal cross you gave me," I explained to Brian. "I hung it in that window, and I thought he broke it kicking his soccer ball in the house. But now I see that the dog must have done it."

"You didn't even believe me. You didn't even listen," Evan said, his eyes flashing with accusation.

I shook my head, my vision growing blurry as tears pooled in my eyes. I had been so unfair. If he couldn't count on his own mother to believe him, who could he count on in life? I had let him down. "No, I didn't. I'm so sorry."

"Yeah, right." He pushed back from the table. "I get my GameBoy back now, don't I?"

"Yes. Yes, of course," I sniffed. What did it matter if I proved myself at the office? I was the worst mother ever.

"Where is it?" Evan demanded in an ugly voice.

"I can't remember," I said brokenly. "I think I put it in—"

"She's not going to tell you where it is until you show her some respect," Brian insisted in a firm deep voice that I'd only heard him use jokingly before. This time he was serious.

"What do you mean?" Evan asked, clearly surprised.

"Look her in the face. Speak to her as you would want her to speak to you. Tell her you accept her apology."

"But this is her fault! She didn't believe me."

"Of course she didn't believe you," Alicia said quickly. "You're always kicking that ball in the house. And you know you're not supposed to."

"But I didn't break the cross."

"We know. And she said she was sorry."

I held up my hand to interrupt. I was grateful that Alicia and Brian had sprung to my defense. But I needed to handle this myself. I took a deep breath and tried to keep my voice steady. I had made a mistake, true. But that did not make me the worst mom ever. Evan had made mistakes as well.

"Look, Evan, I am sorry that I punished you unfairly."

"Okay."

"I made a mistake. But if you look at it from my perspective, you'll see why I didn't believe you. You've told me so many lies lately that I stopped believing anything you said."

He pushed his fork around on his plate but didn't deny anything, which was tantamount to an admission of guilt in my experience.

"I was wrong about this, though," I continued, "and I apologize." I felt like I needed to say something else, but I wasn't sure what it was. When we apologize, we were supposed to admit wrongdoing and pledge to not repeat it in the future. Was there anything else?

I glanced at Brian. When he apologized to me, he asked me to forgive him. I hadn't really understood it at the time. *Forgive* was one of those church words, something we ask God to do all the time. But I guess we're supposed to forgive each other, too. And if you want someone to give you something, it's probably a good idea to ask for it.

"Will you forgive me, Evan?"

He looked at me strangely.

"This is your chance to be like God," Brian prompted. "Say 'yes'."

"Um, yeah sure," Evan mumbled. "I forgive you."

"Thank you." And I would show my gratitude by not running over to hug him, which was what I wanted to do, just like when he was little.

He wouldn't want me to. He didn't see himself as my little boy, and I had to respect that. When he was older, maybe he'd feel okay hugging me again.

Brian reached over to squeeze my hand.

"Well, that's over," Alicia said dismissively. "So, what's for dessert?"

"Yeah," Brian said, his eyes twinkling with mischief. "What's next?"

I didn't know what was next from dessert on. I didn't know whether Brian and I were together forever or only for the next season of extracurricular activities. I didn't know when I would have the next confrontation with one of my kids, but I knew there would be more. I didn't know how I would handle my next case for Dave, or even if there would be any more cases. But I knew that somehow, I would be able to handle whatever was next.

Maybe having God hanging over me all the time like a chaperone wasn't such a bad thing after all.

Like her heroine, K. D. is a "soccer mom" living in an old town that has become a suburb of Baltimore. But unlike her heroine, she is still happily married, active in her church, and visits every historical site she can manage. It took her almost thirty-five years to realize that she had always wanted to be a writer. During those years, she worked at a variety of different jobs, serving as everything from a bookkeeper and preschool teaching assistant to a newspaper columnist, hostess in a hospitality suite at NASCAR races, and corporate attorney for a pest control company. She reports that being a mom is the best job of all, but that writing books runs a close second.

You may correspond with this author by writing:
K. D. Hays
Author Relations
PO Box 721
Uhrichsville, OH 44683

A Letter to Our Readers

Dear Reader:

In order to help us satisfy your quest for more great mystery stories, we would appreciate it if you would take a few minutes to respond to the following questions. We welcome your comments and read each form and letter we receive. When completed, please return to:

Fiction Editor
Heartsong Presents—MYSTERIES!
PO Box 721
Uhrichsville, Ohio 44683

Did you enjoy reading *Worth Its Weight in Old* by K. D. Hays?

Very much! I would like to see more books like this! The one thing I particularly enjoyed about this story was:

_____

_____

_____

Moderately. I would have enjoyed it more if:

_____

_____

_____

Are you a member of the HP—MYSTERIES! Book Club?
◯ Yes ◯ No

If no, where did you purchase this book?

_____

Please rate the following elements using a scale of 1 (poor) to 10 (superior):

___ Main character/sleuth   ___ Romance elements

___ Inspirational theme   ___ Secondary characters

___ Setting   ___ Mystery plot

How would you rate the cover design on a scale of 1 (poor) to 5 (superior)? _____

What themes/settings would you like to see in future **Heartsong Presents—MYSTERIES!** selections? ————
_____
_____
_____

Please check your age range:
- Under 18
- 18–24
- 25–34
- 35–45
- 46–55
- Over 55

Name: _____

Occupation: _____

Address: _____

E-mail address: _____